Operations and Tears

Dedication

I dedicate this anthology to the memory of numerous relatives, friends and colleagues who have died in the past thirty years. Some were carried away by the deadly HIV/AIDS pandemic just when an effective treatment was in sight. May their souls rest in peace.

Published by
Kachere Series
P.O Box 1037, Zomba
ISBN 99908-76-04-5 (Kachere Book no. 16)

Layout: Olive Goba
Cover design: Olive Goba
Graphic design: Patrick Lichakala

Operations and Tears

A New Anthology of Malawian Poetry

Anthony Nazombe

Kachere Book no. 16
Kachere Series
Zomba

Kachere Series
P.O. Box 1037, Zomba, Malawi
kachere@globemw.net
www.sdnp.org.mw/kachereseries

This book is part of the Kachere Series, a range of books on religion, culture and society from Malawi. Other Kachere titles published so far are:

J.C. Chakanza, *Wisdom of the People: 2000 Chinyanja Proverbs*

David Mphande, *Nthanthi za Chitonga za Kusambizgiya ndi Kutauliya*

Pádraig Ó Máille, *Living Dangerously. A Memoir of Political Change in Malawi*

J.W.M. Van Breugel, *Chewa Traditional Religion*

David S. Bone (ed.), *Malawi's Muslims: Historical Perspectives*

James N. Amanze, *African Traditional Religion in Malawi: The Case of the Bimbi Cult*

George Shepperson and Tom Price, *Independent African: John Chilembwe and the Nyasaland Rising of 1915*

Janet Y. Kholowa and Klaus Fiedler, *In the Beginning God Created them Equal*

John McCracken, *Politics and Christianity in Malawi 1875-1940: The Impact of the Livingstonia Mission in the Northern Province*

The Kachere Series is the publications arm of the Department of Theology and Religious Studies of the University of Malawi.

Series Editors: J.C. Chakanza, F.L. Chingota, Klaus Fiedler, P.A. Kalilombe, S. Mahommad, Fulata L. Moyo, Martin Ott.

Acknowledgements

This anthology would not have seen the light of day had it not been for the insistence of several colleagues and friends. After spending a total of five years on the compilation and editing of *The Haunting Wind,* I personally felt I had rendered enough service to Malawi's poets. I thought I could sit back and watch the effects on the local and international audiences. However, I had not reckoned with the pace of social and political change in Malawi. The events of 1992 – 1994 engulfed us all, and we found ourselves participating in a variety of roles. The work of the Chancellor College Writers Workshop, whose progress I had been following from October 1973, reflected the mood of the times, as some of the poems included in the present anthology will show. In addition quite a few of the twenty odd independent newspapers that suddenly appeared on the streets began to carry poetry, and it was fascinating reading, although the quality was rather low. In the face of these momentous changes, Kenneth and Hesther Ross approached me and asked me to put together a representative collection of poems which would appear in the Kachere Series. I had by then a file of poems from the various papers and the anthology title *Poetry and Democracy in Malawi* had already suggested itself. The more I looked at the pieces, however, the more skeptical I became of their lasting appeal. Most of them were really doggerels. It was then that I turned to my Writers' Workshop files. They contained material which went back to 1973, when I joined Chancellor College of the University of Malawi as an undergraduate student. Some of the poems had already found their way into *The Haunting Wind* and into several collections by individual hands. Others had been set aside for an anthology which David Kerr and I were going to edit for Paul Green's Dangerous Writers Series. Yet others had been ear marked for a possible collection entitled *Eyes of the Beholder: Pictures and Poems Reflecting Malawi's Spectacular Beauty.* As I waded through this material as well as through some of the books authored by the founding members of the Writers' Group/Writers' Workshop, I found the scope of the project broadening. I would compile a companion piece or a sequel to *The Haunting Wind* which would contain some new efforts as well as work which had been previously difficult to come by. Some of it would, in fact, have been rejected

5

outright by the Censorship Board. In other words, I was going to take full advantage the utterly changed socio-political atmosphere.

Operations and Tears has had a gestation period of some seven years. During that time its size and shape have changed considerably. `This has been in large part due to my editorial qualms. As I read and reread the manuscript, I found that some of the poems I had originally included did not quite fit into the overall pattern that was gradually emerging or they were not taut enough. I did not hesitate to remove them and to replace them with others. Again, as had been the case with the composition of *The Haunting Wind*, I was worried about the paucity of verse by women writers. Some useful suggestions in this connection came from Ms Fiona Chalamanda in Great Britain. To her I am deeply grateful. The Vice Chancellor of the University of Malawi, Professor David Rubadiri, gently intervened when the prospective publishers felt that the compilation was taking a bit too long. Ms Alison McFarlane, who spent nine months with the Department of English at Chancellor College, also added a sense of urgency to the operation. Directly or indirectly, she has contributed to the refinement of the final product.

I turn now to the specific credits. The poems by Hoffman Aipira were given to me by the author himself when I met him in York, England, in 1997. He was introduced to me by the exiled Malawian poet, Jack Mapanje. Innocent Banda's contribution somehow found its way into my Writers' Workshop files. The piece by Sai Bwanali had been discussed in the Writers' Workshop. Steve Chimombo kindly made the poems included here available to me. Some had previously appeared in his magazine, *WASI,* and at least one, *'Beggar Woman',* was first published in his 1987 collection, *Napolo Poems.* Frank Chipasula's: *'The Struggle for Independence'* and *'Makoha'* were taken from his pioneering volume, *Visions and Reflections.* The remainder of the poems came from *O Earth, Wait for Me.* Except for *'Referendum'*, which I read on the BBC, the poems by Zangaphee Chizeze appeared mistakenly under my name in the anthology *New Accents One*, edited by Stanley Nyamfukudza and brought out by the College Press in Harare, Zimbabwe. The pieces by S.E. Chiziwa, Catherine Duclos and Dunstan Gausi were all on file. Cecilia Hasha's *'A Woman's Cry'* was borrowed from *WASI.* Maxford Iphani's two pieces and Gustave Kaliwo's *'… Into the Wilderness'* are Writers' Workshop fare. I am indebted to David Kerr for providing me with the four poems printed here. Kapwepwe Khonje's two compositions and Joji Ngoto Kumwenda's 'Limbo' will be remembered from the Writers' Workshop discussions. I would like to thank my student, Monica Brenda Kumwenda, for supplying me with the two

6

poems included here. The five contributions by Ken Lipenga came from my file. John Lwanda kindly permitted me to publish the two poems here through his sister, Chipo Kanjo. The poems by Jack Mapanje came from two volumes of his, namely, *Of Chameleons and Gods* and *The Chattering Wagtails of Mikuyu Prison*. I had hoped to include some pieces from his *Skipping Without Ropes* but a student who borrowed my copy of the book knew better than I and never bothered to return it to me. Such is the hunger for books in Malawi. The compositions of Zeleza Manda and Alfred Matiki came from my file. Zondiwe Mbano kindly placed the five efforts included here at my disposal. As a matter of interest, *'Beware, Millipede'* is one of the few good poems inspired by the political transition of 1992-1994. Both Rowland Mbvundula and M. Mkandawire are represented by Writers' Workshop material. The unusually large body of poetry by Felix Mnthali has been culled, with his tacit approval, from his *When Sunset Comes to Sapitwa,* of which two editions exist, one Zambian and the other British. As for Francis Moto's four contributions, they came from his collection, *Gazing at the Setting Sun*, brought out by Fegs Publications. The poems anticipate the changeover from single party to multiparty rule. Lupenga Mphande's poems go back a long way. The lengthy piece by Edison Mpina was specially requested by this editor. J.J. Msosa's poems mysteriously found their way into this writer's possession. My thanks go to Khumbula Munthali, Ian Musowa, Sam Raiti Mtamba and Geoff Mwanja for supplying the poems printed here. Anthony Nazombe's pieces are from an unpublished collection entitled *The Racket and Other Poems*. A garbled version of *'Blind Terror'* appeared in *The Lamp*. *'Song for a Hunter'* was published in *Us/THEM: Translation, Transcription and Identity in Post-Colonial Literary Cultures*, edited by Gordon Collier and brought out by Editions Rodopi in Amsterdam and Atlanta, and *'Battle for Chingwe's Hole'* was included in an issue of *Outlook* edited by Steve Chimombo. Alfred Tyson Nkhoma and Immanuel Bofomo Nyirenda are familiar voices from the Writers' Workshop in Zomba. I am grateful to Patrick O' Malley for making the three poems here available to me. For the reader's information, *'For Us Who Remain'*, written after Jack Mapanje's detention on 25th September, 1987, was withdrawn from circulation by the Chancellor College administration. I discovered the Nigerian writer Niyi Osundare's dedicatory poem in an issue of the African Literature Association (ALA) bulletin which had been sent to me, obviously as a gesture of solidarity, during Mapanje's incarceration. My thanks go to D.B.V. Phiri for supplying the three poems printed here. The pieces by Kadwa Phungwako and Ambokile Salimu were taken from Writers'

Workshop files. I am grateful to the expatriates Francis Sefe, Edwin Segal and Landeg White for entrusting me with their creative work. The pieces by White were taken from the volumes *For Captain Stedman* and *A View from the Stockade.*

Finally, I am deeply thankful to the staff of the Kachere Series for undertaking to publish these poems. Whatever flaws there are in the twin processes of selection and editing are mine alone.

Anthony Joseph Mukomele Nazombe: Zomba, November, 2003

Contents

Waterfall
Hoffman Aipira

at the southern tip
lake Malawi shrinks
to a tit
squirting its cargo
into the River Shire

here the language changes
everything is up for grabs
fishing rods lurk in the waters
for the right moment
a dead chambo ashore
stranded brings
vultures claw to claw

clever bits of wood
iron and steel across
the water-divide
even hollowed-out logs
oversell their stamina
surfing over swirling waters
antagonised Hippos dread

imposing territorial rule
on trafficking canoes
on the river delta
crickets flirt on rock pimples
frogs chant another
sunset in mudpools
trees of Heaven

vegetate to the sky
aping majestic
mountain peaks
down and beyond

facing a narrow corridor
foaming river banks meet
ready to roar
waterfall

dad
Hoffman Aipira

take the hoe my son
carefully tie the seed-bag
at the end of the hoe-handle
at the first light
before the dew is dry
mark a patch of soil
to carry this seed
and give life
hope

drought
Hoffman Aipira

it is
no exaggeration
your silence
is more eloquent
than words
here
clouds
are unwilling
to deposit
seasonal tears
on us

why
scatter
more seeds
in crowded
ridges
wearing
contorted faces
watching obese
earth worms
in compost heaps
releasing fertility
detained
in fertilisers
for an Eden

denied

distant drums
Hoffman Aipira

look at these masked dancers
in rugged regalia

trooping out of their dambwe
to the melodies of distant drums

talking in tongues we will never know
but evoking strong passion from the initiated

it's been like, this for generations
Whoever is uninitiated in their traditional rites

must stay away lest they face ruthless axes
have you thought for a while, Naomi?

have you wondered why there is
initiation for our survival?

here we are in the cracking heat of the savannah
this kitchen our hideout. Hold your nerve,

steady on, Naomi, hold the child
as the masked dancers under the cool ambience

of a baobab tree leave the air pregnant
with sweat and dust dancing the big dance

The Last Respects
Hoffman Aipira

Death falls on sudden wings
and a graveyard plays host
to faces of anguish,
eyes watching fingers
tears rolling
forming patterns
on sagging chins.

In the midst of solemnity
a village priest mutters the last rites
as the deceased exits
to a callous void
without best wishes.
From a tired ember sky
a fading face of the sunset
observes
shovels and spades
attacking earth mounds
burying difficult times.

New Cities, New Landscapes
Hoffman Aipira

The globe fast forwards
to a massive construction site
temples of brick and mortar
speaking in landmarks
emerging cities -
a concrete jungle
asserting itself.

The fizzy voice of celebration
pops out champagne bottles
an icing on ribbon cutting rituals
handshakes and mouth-wide grins.

Somewhere on the globe
cranes and shovels
club together in union
like promiscuous earth diggers
lifting up with rising expectations
on virgin lands.

Falling on the debris
generous heavens disperse
drizzly rains
like friendly arsenals
torturing our senses
with dry scent of cement.

Those who care
about green
notice anorexic trees
tottering
into ubiquitous
skyline gasping for air

a mature forest nearby
grunts
shedding leaves
before the autumn fall.

Not I
Hoffman Aipira

Weren't you born at noon
in the lunar year of the horse
a tiny body
kicking and screaming
a vigorous statement
of your arrival
wearing out
your mother's patience
in the tropical heat
of October sun?

Didn't you boast
about intercepting
a viper lunging
at an absent-minded
rodent for its midday meal
fishing in rivers
teeming with crocodiles
and beating a path through
thorny acacia bushes?

Didn't you trek
across mighty Zambezi
thirsting for a better future
endure freezing winters overseas
for more letters after your name?

Could it be you now
wearing worried looks
staring at the world
with negative confidence
and in difficulty coordinating
speech and thought?

Not I.

A Letter from Abroad
Hoffman Aipira

It's winter here
the season of snowman
and minor avalanches
on rooftops. Tenacious winds
hold your breath and the sun
illuminates but it does not warm.

Rows of litter bags
queue with bulging frustration,
yawning beer bottles
cuddle in the biting cold
telling a story of weekend blues
in the flat above.

Endless cold and flu
make this place a pharmacist's dream
but the distance invokes nostalgia -
the lingering smell of smoked Kampango
back home never left me.

Imagine living in ice-age
imagine beans on toast and guinness on tap
breaking the ice in conversations.
Imagine that.

Mix and Match
Hoffman Aipira

Look at these superhighways
On desktops, post-modern towers
Mushrooming and choicest palate
Onto dinner tables gobbled
By gold-plated false teeth.

This is the new world
Lighting candles here, casting shadows there
And there:

Caviar lingering under silver chandeliers
Alacarte meals wafting aromatic scents
And well cropped chins jutting out
In bold aftershave - Not a sniff.

Chinaware made-to-order
Crockery on a bed of velvet serviettes
And diamonds glittering - Not in sight.

Of the craftsmen in chef hats
Tending pans of crispy salads
And flaming grills shouldering rare steaks -
Only hard work
Heat and overtime.

For the Grand old Man
(Dedicated to Prof. David Rubadiri)
Kisa Amateshe

Thy princely presence overshadows
The Mighty Zomba Mountain-
You sagely sit in poetic style
As you speak in lyrical rhythms

Holding us captive of your baritone:
Words weaved in euphony,
Gentle laughters in between
The tales of far-away lands.

Thy relentless eyes reveal
Pains of a derailed history
 As you tearfully recount
Years of 'African Thunderstorms.'

Yet we still happily laugh,
Gentle laughters of our reunion:
You, our mentor, taking us
Through the labyrinth of life.

We can feel the melodious music
Of the many songs you have sung
And the timelessness of your art
In global galleries of the world.

We feel your stately presence
At the creative milestones-
Your works graciously walking
With silent strides to eternity!

What other songs shall we sing
To celebrate this, our reunion,
In this haven by the Mountain?
What other styles shall we dance?

Still the grand old man

Remains the master story-teller,
Holding us captive of his greatness
As the night gently falls on Zomba.
When will tomorrow return?

Man Eater Go!
Innocent Banda

In leaf the trees are beautiful
Beautiful blades of grass break the earth;
Any type of cloud is hopeful on dry days
These scattered showers over there are full of hope.
Everything everything is beautiful here except for the
Pain in the eyes of children puzzled with hunger,
Everything except for the liars keen to build granaries
With forked tongues.

Poverty smiling, stares vacantly like gaping graves
Printed in the eye-holes of a smiling skeleton
Full toothed, wry and evil.

These sparkling cars are washed in human blood,
Skin-dried and polished with human brains;
These three piece suits are soaked in the tears
Of the beer-pot bellies double rimmed chins
Could flesh a million skeletons disposed at birth
Or better swell the empty milk sacks flapping
The dry chests of nursing mothers.

A baby died in the village, did you burn any milk
Or fill up an automobile tank? Have you tapped your foot
To the crying of babies, hummed a tune in harmony with
Convulsive gulps or cracked the joke of the century
Of the poor in rigor mortis?

Fat man go jump off Sapitwa,
Seven headed dragon your apocalypse is at your tail
Trees, grass, clouds and rain, in this beauty
You begot the beasts that eat obsequious 'flower' children
Man Eater Go!
Which dark sea gave you birth?

This Family
Sai Bwanali

This family of ours has a father.
We are many in this family
But we have been told
By our father that we are all one.
Are we really one?

Our father has lust
for honour though he
Has been honoured for years now.

But what happened a few years ago
Was very dishonorable.
You remember our elder brothers
Who wanted to help us see the light?
What happened to them,
All of us know.

Father, I am the last born
But if there comes a step father,
I will readily accept him
And if he proves himself
Not fatherly, then we will look
For another since we
Cannot come back to you.

Will it be because of age
Or because of the way
You are going to leave
This family?
I wonder.

Honour father;
Is it what you are fathering us for?
Born only to be honoured?
I wonder.

A Nation of Corpses
Steve Chimombo

We inherited a country of corpses
Not financial losses or devaluations.
We reel under the flotation of cadavres
Not of the Kwacha or the tambala,
As we auction off coffin-loads of dead.

Exchanging the number of lately dead,
Is now the local currency, as we enter
The AIDS victims' figure in our forex
To be wired to international aid organizations
For our foreign reserves to accumulate.

We got rid of the pollution of dictatorship
But let loose pestilences on the population.
Now itinerant HIV and cholera demand
A corpse or two from each household
Not the notorious party card of old.

We do not need Napolo or Phalombe disasters.
We survived those, and the army worms, too,
And the crocodile farms for political dissidents.
Our awiro are now overfed, bloated nalimvimvi
Welcoming terminal cases to the graveyards.

Fateful footsteps pound the corridors
To meet empty offices vacated temporarily
For an appointment with a mchape doctor.
Swirling dust storms are not raised by dancing feet
But hurried departures to rendez-vous with death.

When it is not funeral bearers we meet
Rebounding on the potholes of our tarred roads,
It is grave-scarred faces we encounter
Returning from spirit-ridden medicinemen
Brewing concoctions over the polluted village air.

When truckloads of returning mourners
Meet in head-on collisions with busloads
Of funeral goers, the excess dead cannot
Be buried in the usual graves anymore,
Not when we can export the cadavres.

Our national annual budgets are computed
with the lucrative in the corpses
With our less fortunate foreign neighbours
Across the border for their medical colleges.
This is part of our poverty alleviation programme.

Pyagusi
Steve Chimombo

(James Frederick Sangala,
Founder of the Nyasaland African Congress)

I

You were another Chameleon
Wearing different names, too
Like Nanzikambe, Tonkhwetonkhwe,
Birimankhwe, or even Kalilombe.

You were "Pyagusi" the performer,
"J.F." to those who revered you,
And Mr Sangala to those unsure of you:
Politician, businessman, counsellor in one.

Whether Chinangwa Farm or Kaphirintiwa,
Your homes were the same: refuge or shrine,
Taking in an orphan here, or paying out fees there,
Naming a child here, or arbitrating a dispute there.

Now you survive only in consanguinity:
"Malume," paternal links to others,
"Baba," paternal links to others,
"Ambuye," grandfather to them all.

II

They no longer mention you,
In these days of instant politics,
Obliterated by heady multipartyism
And the bitter-sweet taste of democracy.

They did not mention you even then,
At the advent of the first independence,
Obscured by incipient African despotism,
Flung into the wings of deluded nationalism.

Kamuzuism, pseudo politics, broke your back.
And you retreated to Kaphirintiwa,
The birth place of all mankind,
And, I would say, the African Congress.

You lie in St. Michael's and All Angels, your church.
They should have built you a monument
Called Mute Martyrs of Dictatorship
And all Related Victims of Bandaism.

Advice to Mbona the Prophet

Steve Chimombo

When you visit us again
Through your medium, Mlauli,
Eyes almost popping out
Mouth white with slaver
Voice what you have to prophesy

Do not turn your back on us
When we say we know already
What message you bring us.

There will be drought, you shout.
There is one already in our midst
As devastating as the one last year.
Even the sacred pools are now dry
You can count the cracked crabshells
Lying at the bottom of the caked moss.

There will be famine, you cry.
You can see the hundreds dying
Like falling leaves in late summer
Emaciated grey skins peeling off
Ribs sticking out like unfinished rafters
Mass graves we open everyday.

There will be pandemics, you scream
This is no great news really, we say,
What with the cholera victims joining
The AIDS and HIV positives in our midst
After the malaria compounded with meningitis.

There will be pestilences, you yell louder.
But this comes belatedly to the survivors
who used to eat the red locusts before.
But the new armyworms are not digestible
Ensuring that punishment comes not with comfort.

Spare us your prophetic madness, Mbona,
Convulsive fits, and penitential flagellations
All stating the obvious truth invading us
Living in our midst and decimating us
As we will spare you the only libations left
Since we can no longer afford the flour.

Speak instead of a world without dread
Though we cannot image what we
Will be like without our familiar afflictions.

A Death Song

Steve Chimombo

> (Birimankhwe maso adatupa ninji?
> Kwathu maliro
> Msamaseke ana inu;
> Kwayera mbee, mbee, mbee
>
> Ine n'dzachoka pam'dzi pano;
> Mutsale mumange pam'dzipano.
> Taonani pakhomo pangapa:
> Payera, mbee, mbee, mbee.)

I

> (Chameleon, why are your eyes swollen?
> There's death at home.)

The chameleon was wrong.
The tear stricken swollen
Swivelling eyes did not see
The lizard still scuttling
On the potsherds of Kaphirintiwa
Did not hear the Kalilombe's
Survival song as she burst open
To give birth to laughter, song and dance.

Yes, the locusts came
And joined the army worms
And the monkeys in the middle
Of the maize, beans and groundnuts gardens
But the west brought aids
And hybrid maize to replenish
The ravished sturdy local stock.
The east brought yaws too
In nice neat rice packets
And the media promised us
Another bumper harvest because
Of the prevailing peace and prosperity.

II

(Look at my homestead:
It's empty, empty, empty.)

The chameleon was wrong
The homestead was not really empty.
Some zombies were left
In spite of their deafness.
The ndondochas wailed at night
Despite their tongues being cut off.
They were not yet completely dead.

Yes carloads of souls
Met their sticky ends
At the end of the line.
However the survivors were permitted
To attend the funerals and burials
Under careful supervision.

III

(I shall leave this village
You stay behind and build the village)

The chameleon was wrong
The answer was not to abandon the village
As rats do a sinking ship
Or fleas a dying hedgehog.
Exile, pretended, genuine
Or self-imposed is not the answer
To the holocaust or the apocalypse.
Yes, we seek new homes everyday
The old ones no longer habitable.
We hunt for new myths everywhere
The ancient ones defeated or defiled
However, recycled homes or myths
Are better than nothing
they are all we have left.

IV

(Do not laugh, children
It's empty, empty, empty.)

You are wrong, chameleon
Just look at the survivors
How many Nyanjas did not hurtle
Heading into Chingwe's Hole?
How many Ngonis did not
Partake of the kalongonda?
How many Chewas were not
Crushed at Mpata-wa-Milonde?
How many Kafulas did not
Suffocate in the Bunda caves?

Yes, you are wrong chameleon
Just count how many delayed
their deaths in spite of the lizard's message
Look how laughter, song dance
Still rebound against the rock
Of Kaphirintiwa:
We are still alive!

Beggar Woman
Steve Chimombo

1

And will the lice,
having intimations of my death,
flee from my body
like rats abandon a sinking ship
or fleas a dying hedgehog?

I have felt my hair - that lush breeding ground-
stand on its toes to make hairways and highways
for flatulent bellies of overfed lice and unhatched eggs.

The eggs hatch into little ones,
the little lice grow into big ones,
and they all suck my soul.
play hide-and suck on cloth and hair.

They have coursed the great forests of my hair,
created the well-beaten pathways of tiny feet,
clawing and gorging their way through the tufts.

The black ones claim my head,
the light-skinned ones my body.
The glinting patches, the bloody spotches,
the skeletons are all signs of their progress.

And alone at night I have recorded their work songs,
these humming wonderworkers draining my life-blood,
felt the caress of prowling feet and the love bites.

The syncopation of hunting feet,
the gush of blood form the unlucky,
another louse dead.
The explosion of a swatted louse:
die, louse, die.

Single-handed I have fought titanic battles in my rags,
nightly unleashed imprecations, fingers, and fingernails
at vanguards, and horde after horde, of gigantic lice.

Lean-bellied militants and revolutionaries,
the riot squad and iron-jawed warriors,
reading the Declaration of Lice Rights:
the right to live on unclaimed territory.

And I have woken up in the mornings ululating,
counted my conquests like I count my daily takings
of genocidal nights from the folds of my cloth.

I have peeled, scraped, and wiped off
blotched carcasses, mangled corpses,
raged at the giant blobs of blood,
the smear of lice juice on black skin.

What they want from me, a withered beggar woman,
what they want from the shrivelled dugs, I don't know,
surely they can find juicier conquests out there?

On affluent streets, in carpeted offices,
the teeming buses, the gutting planes,
the Toyotas, the Benzes, the Royces,
the Titanic, the Ilala, the Queen Elizabeth?

Surely there are more choice parts,
jewelled arms, powdered pits, breasts,
perfumed underwear and petticoats
to play games of hide-and-suck in?

Yielding bellies on sumptuous beds,
succulent bottoms on feathered mattresses,
shampooed hair in air-conditioned hotels,
are these not for you and yours too?

II

I can no longer count the sighs and tear drops
on my bloodstained fingernails and chirundu,
nor can I weigh songs and laughter frozen in me
by the scars and fresh wounds of my ragged soul;
too much blood has flowed already to mingle
with myriad lies and dismembered hopes;
many lives have abandoned truckloads of promises.

When the stomach cannot share
the blood the heart has pumped,
the stomach turns upon itself
and feeds upon its own sweat.

I have wrested the beatitudes from the preacher's lips,
thunderbolted them into the teeth of the whirlwind,
and watched double-headed worms transmogrifying;
for I, too, have been to the mountain top in my chirundu,
have felt the rock of Kaphirintiwa on my bare feet;
for I, too, have paid my dues at Msinja and Nsanje,
And have walked trunks of dreams under each arm.

I crouch here in a thicket of ashes,
forging words and lives,
forging the past and the future,
forging the present.

I retrieve from the embers scarred and charred ends
of napalm-coated words, fractured lives and pasts,
atomized futures and presents melting here and now
I cool them with sighs and tears of brothers and sisters
and fling them, sizzling conundrums, exploding
or rebounding on the granite-faced rock of Kaphirintiwa,
but I hear only cremated echoes of radioactive skeletons.

Echoes of images salvaged
from disremembered shrines;
metaphors of other timeless forges
that weld our present and our future.

III

What the elders said is true;
When the rain sees your dirt,
especially with lice too,
it does not stop.
Yet she who has espoused lightning
does not fear the flashes.

I have seen many rains too:
Napolo found me in the streets,
I sought sanctuary in the shops,
the offices, the church, the school,
but they had all put up the sign:
'Trespassers Will Be Persecuted,'
so I walked into the teeth of Napolo,
to a lonely and ancient nsolo tree;
I knelt, trembling, in the mud,
and washed my bloodstained chirundu;
naked, I squeezed lice between my fingers:
between fingernail and fingernail.
Blood, rain, and tears washed over me
and ran in torrents downhill.
I cleansed the knotted corners of my soul,
clogged by lice and clusters of lice eggs;
I shook my hair loose and hurled off

soot, ashes, bats' droppings, and lice;
and my womb quickened with dirges.
I watched torsoes of lizards, squashed mice,
entrails of chameleon and cockroach shells
eddying in the whirlpools around me.
And at every lightning flash I could see
the upturned faces of drowned varmints
in the gutters, the sewers, the streams,
swirling past the shops, offices, church doors.
Every lightning flash illuminated me
 and the havoc my god had wreaked:
dismembered phantoms from Napolo's menagerie
frothing and surging in the furious vortex.

    In the aftermath of Napolo,
    I emerge from the chaosis
    and march down rainbathed pavements
    singing on the fingernails of the rainbow.

Developments from the Grave

Steve Chimombo

I

We have come full circle,
it seems: burying our dead
right in the homestead now,
on the sites the living had built,

We no longer bury our corpses
over there and away from us,
overhung by weeping nkhadzi trees
just as the missionaries advised us.

We have come full circle,
at last: burying our dead
deep in the soil beneath us;
we climb over the mounds daily.

We no longer hang the cadavers
high in the trees away from scavengers:
hyenas, ants, beaks and talons;
just as the colonials instructed us.

2

We brought the dead to the homestead,
revived them as ndondocha,
cut off their tongues and tamed them
to live in our granaries forever.

Bumper harvests come out of them
and we know who keeps the most,
organising them into one task force
to labour in the tobacco, tea and cotton estates.

We unearthed the youth for msendawana
to skin them for their precious leather
and made purses out of the tender skin
for the most petent charm of them all.

We know who has the largest purse
accumulating wealth, and more.
Out of the mounds of our youth
sprout palaces, fleets and monuments.

3

Development did not catch us
by surprise, asleep or unprepared:
We knew about space exploration:
we had our own flying baskets.

The greenhouse effect is not news;
we know how to heat or cool the land:
Drought comes from a society on heat;
rain comes from a cooled nation.

But development came from the graves,
too full and closely packed to grow any more.
The protective nkhadzi trees fenced
each effort to force the grave boundaries.

We have now come full circle,
rightly so: living with our dead,
not only in nsupa or spirit houses
but in granaries, purses and coffins.

A Love Poem for My Country
For James
Frank Chipasula

I have nothing to give you, but my anger
And the filaments of my hatred reach across the border.
You, you have sold many and me to exile.
Now shorn of precious minds, you rely only on
What hands can grow to build your crumbling image.

Your streets are littered with handcuffed men.
And the drums are thuds of the warden's spiked boots.
You wriggle with agony as the terrible twins, law and order
Call out the tune through the thick tunnels of barbed wire.

Here, week after week, the walls dissolve and are slim,
The mist is clearing and we see you naked like
A body that is straining to find itself but cannot
And our hearts are thumping with pulses of desire or fear
And our dreams are charred chapters of your history.

My country, remember I neither blinked nor went to sleep;
My country, I never let your life slide downhill
And passively watched you, like a recklessly driven car,
Hurrying to your crash, while the driver leapt out.

The days have lost their song and salt
We feel bored without our free laughter and voice
Every day thinking the same and discarding our hopes.
Your days are loud with clanking cuffs
On men's arms as they are led away to decay.

I know a day will come and wash away my pain
And I will emerge from the night breaking into song
Like the sun, blowing out these evil stars.

Tikambepo
Frank Chipasula

Unmailable letter to Jack Mapanje
(I know this poem will not unlock the prison gate)

and our greatest
hope
will be to find out
next year
that they're still torturing him
eight months later

Today the devil bird lays
your hard-boiled brain
in a barbed-wire nest
where your manacled thoughts
moulder behind concrete
walls and steel bars,
you who went to tune your crude
bangwe in a cold foreign land
and return home where dogs
sniffed your footprints
for secret pulses of revolt
in your secret arteries where
lust and erotic blood burned
for your lover, your land
naked before you.
with a cudgel they try to extract
a speck from your keen eye
that saw the specks in theirs!
Ah! brother, we must go to school
again about life, I know:
They misunderstood you when you
called for Mercy, you called for your wife,
And Courage you called your daughter.
And Courage we call to your side.
15 November 1988

We Must Crush the Parasite
After Pablo Neruda
Frank Chipasula

We must hunt that parasite, the pest,
until we crush him under our boots;
smoke him out of his hill-hewn palace
into which his desire for death has driven him.
Either stone him down his self-made prison
Down the luminous dungeon or snuff him out,
And let him writhe in the scorching sun.
We must spray him with terrible bullets of verse,
This skunk who has made dark and shady
Transactions with the enemy and sold our land;
Bombard this thing till it is tattered like a rag:
This flea, this swollen jigger, this parasite
lodged to the neck with our pilfered blood.
We must fearlessly dig our own flesh
and root him out of his secret hide-out;
Hook him out by his shrivelled wasp legs
Swaddled in the London worsted,
Flush out this parasite that wears the image
of a benevolent lion stained with our blood:
Grab his false tail and chop off
his long claws that have strangled our land,
that have reached every hut and snuffed out the fire.
We must grab him by his false tail
and brain him against Mulanje mountain.
We must be ready with our sharpened pens and inkwells
filled with the blood he has siphoned from our veins
and splash his huge sin all over his overcoat.
We must be ready with hard-hitting couplets
angry with double hatred, furious with love,
tercets exploding with thrice the violence
of this terrible lion.

We must load them with monstrous images
of fierce grotesque lizards always ready to strike.
We shall train our polished steel muzzles on him,
let the hand grenades of flaming metaphors
get him right in the gut, and ravage this handful of dust.
We must rout this terrible Chitute today.
We must crush this parasite today.

Providence, RI: November 1982 and 8 April 1983

The Struggle for African Independence

Frank Chipasula

I awoke one morning
Into shouts of 'Freedom!!!'
Queer, I thought.
Being only a boy, I didn't take it in.
'Kwacha' I knew meant dawn,
But dawn was there every morning.
Why shout it out then?
Something's wrong, I thought.
'Uhuru!!!' I heard but
I knew not what it meant!
Everywhere were angry faces,
Protests were the order of the day,
People ran about with clubs and spears,
Stones and broken glass scattered.
Everywhere there was blood! bloodshed!
Terror reigned in my heart
And I wanted to run away, but ...
I became crazy, picked up
A stone and threw it at
The white District Commissioner's car
And glass broke and I shouted
'Kwacha!! Freedom!!' unconsciously!

I joined the crowd.
We cut down telephone lines,
We put road-barriers everywhere.
The police shot a cloud of smoke
At our eyes and tears streamed
Down my cheeks but never stopped.
They shot down many people but
It didn't work; the fight continued!
There was this man I admired most,
He came and stood on the platform
And encouraged us to fight on:
'Fight on for your freedom, comrades!
This is our fight but fight on

Without violence!
For your child and those that are yet
to be born, fight on with me.
Fight on the front ranks.
They will kill you but don't falter!
We shall shed blood for our freedom!
Without work why should we eat?
We are in their chains but
We won't bear it, and won't give in!'
He shouted, sweat on his temples:
They took our land
And threw us, sons and daughters of this soil,
Out. But we've awakened though
They sealed our eyes!
They wouldn't allow us
To buy from the whites' shops,
Just because we are black!
No colour-bar here, in our own motherland!
Fight on! fight on! Comrades,
Your reward, freedom, you'll have restored
To you. It's your birthright. Kwacha! Freedom!
We all shouted Kwacha! Freedom! Uhuru!
This man smiled and waved happily.

This man I admired
Made journeys to the white man's land
And verbally demanded and claimed
His country's freedom and independence.
They made him sign papers
And he returned with freedom
Safely carried in his coat-pocket!
The white man's flag was lowered.
The raising of our own land's flag
Made me feel freedom in my bones,
In my blood. Yes! in my body.
I trembled and quietly wept for
Those who'd fought but would
Never taste the good fruits of freedom.
Was I free, really? Yes. Free all over!!

It happened in the North, East
And here in the Centre.
Part of Africa's free!

Yet the struggle goes on,
In the South, East, West
And elsehere on the African soil.
Let's all help acquire
Freedom for all Africa!
Brother and sister, freedom's
Our birthright!

The Nature of our Fear

Frank Chipasula

In my country people do not sleep
They keep their curtains open
They fear burglars may break into their dreams
They fear nightmares of monsters in their sleep.

In the streets the people talking
Look over their shoulders from time to time
They do not know why, yet they look at
no one listening to their exchange of greetings.

They do not talk behind closed windows
with curtains drawn they do not sleep;
burglars may break into their nightmares.
People do not sleep in my country.

My people clap hands when they hear lies
My people sing and dance when whips crack their backs.

They are peaceful, they know the law and its long arms,

And the arms of the law drag them through mud.

Yet they stamp their anger into the dust
and their song fills their throats and flows over;
their song is carried on the wind into bird lungs.
And the birds' tears cannot be seen in the rain.

Yet when they sing about Chilembwe: 1915
there is no trace of pain in their voices;
When they sing of his courage even the land trembles
and they no longer look over their shoulders.

The Blind Marimba Player
for Sterling A. Brown
Frank Chipasula

He gathered us, an insane haphazard audience,
Deaf-mutes all, fondled us between the shining metal tips

Whose rusty stem the copper wire held captive to plank
And the well schooled thumb tips, precariously at first,
The fingers embracing, caressing softly the dark oily board
Hurling us up to hazy heavens, whipping us around

The melody went suddenly beserk slapping trees and huts
Breathing into forgotten graves resurrecting the spirits
Of our ancestors, dancing them toying us accusing us
Between the words mouthed on his lips and the morose
Groans of the marimba soundboard, vibrating;
The searching fingers wanting the touch, groping coaxing notes.

The contact did almost everything, though
The player, having made it his magic gourd now
Food-producing coming first on priorities, would stare blankly

Penetrating the target, even piercing my mind
Until another coin, at least another metal piece
Round, the shape came naturally clear on the dark screen in his mind,
Would fall tossed into his rough palm like waste into a bin.

He loved the cold touch with a sly smile;
Then he would unfold before us all the miseries
The cruelties man commits against man in this world
His swift fingers like a millipede train chasing a rare
Tune along the metal bars, his song calling out to dancers
Making them gyrate on thorns and sucking off their tears.

The *marimba* never antagonised him, his sole companion
In his creative protest: he coddled it, his proctor
Who never shared the banana the fingers peeled later
(Only the smear left on its broad by his belly-smacking fingers)

54

Not that it never interested him.
He knew the stroke that satisfied him
The assuring note that took him an octave higher into paradise
And he longed always for that out of the long rehearsals
So he could get it honed, potent to whisper the eternal questions,
The troubles to the player who, nodding, shaking his head

in agony comprehending now facing the opaque skies,
knew all the responses and dutifully answered in chorus singing both his
intimate, inured companion's and his own,
inveighing us who, amused, tragically gave out waves of laughter.

But I, attentive, watched him strum the sweet past
Touch the present momentarily, letting the threads of rhythm
Grope for the truth and proceed violently almost bringing down heaven
To challenge us fill in the dark gaping blanks, like pupils,
Where the future shoul be.

He might have had
The power of sight once: he sang of suffering, torture, hatred.
May be he had had sight, maybe in his childhood
Which he had misused. Perhaps an enemy in blind senseless rage
Had deprived him of his right, the right to see,
And yet now he saw and saw beyond vision.

Or...he had now resigned
Into blindness to his advantage, to strike comfortably
Without sympathy, from his blind spot, a hard more calculated blow-
And we left: one by one the message like a hot pellet
Embedded deep half-forgotten behind the reminding scar.

But I, I carry my *marimba* player in these lines
Guiding him at pole-end as I often did in infancy
My grandfather proudly displaying his honest blindness.

Warrior
for David, and Derek Walcott

Frank Chipasula

Imitation warrior
in synthetic monkey skins

over a three-piece suit
inevitable overcoat, stick,

homburg hat, dark glassed
and false toothed smiles,

he clutched horse-hair
flywhisk and plastic spears

at conference tables in Whitehall
fighting with words only

begging his masters for a new name.
a flag and a new anthem.

'Out of your people's skins
fashion a flag, their bones a flagpole;

Their laments shall be your anthem;
Rename the country and it shall be.'

That is the recipe of his rule
sincere to the last instruction.

of bullets, littering their
mangled bodies like trash

all over our country. Over them
he preached non-violence, forgiveness

and the masters, relieved, curled up
in bed and slept without headaches.

Now he prances clumsily among survivors
mourning their kin at his rallies

as he samples the men for export
to the deep dungeons of Joni

on loan and aid agreements
for the bribe of blood rends.

He demands handclaps
everywhere he turns he confronts

his inflated portraits
nailed and hoisted on flagpoles

Whose blood-drenched banners
are birds straining at ropes.

Corrugated mist like fish scales
covers the eyes of the praise

dancers round him dancing for
the war lost to the settlers.

Then the songs shore up his lofty
platform as he leaves his people

at its foot, steeled with spears
and shields praising the deserter.

They hail him Messiah, Saviour
as he fattens on larceny.

Mahoka (A prayer)
Frank Chipasula

Achibooka, we call you
Excuse us
For you are the lord
This beer we pray you sweeten
and let it not be forsaken.

Akumulungu, we ask you
In this beer you
Ought not to bathe
Hear us
For the lake's free for you.

Achimwenje, we beseech thee
Gather for us a crowd of customers
To buy and feast on this beer
Let them make merry here.

Akumizimu, awake to our cries
Turn to us up there
And behold our suffering
Communicate with the Lord;
At his feet lay this load
Of prayer we beseech you accept.

Father, o grandfathers!
If it's salt or beer or fish
You want from us
We beseech you pray for us;
gladly we shall offer them to you.

She pours libations
to the invisible
ancestral spirits of long dead forefathers
And invokes
The long dead 'ambuyes'
To accept the offering.

For rain
Good health
Or harvest
for good seasons she does it;
'mahoka'

Referendum
Zangaphee Chizeze

In the season
    of the referendum
there is no fear;

Only the echo
    of past terrors
and the mirage
of a bloodied future;

In the season
    of the referendum
there is no rain;

Only the anger
    of a relentless drought
and the vengeance
of storms unchained;

In the season
    of the referendum
there is no time.

Only the endless toil
    of men too tired to rest
and the grief of millions
too hungry to eat;

In the season
    of the referendum
there is no corpse
that flees putrefaction.

To Vince Johns
Zangaphee Chizeze

messages smuggled
through the cordon
of barbwire;
    messages
that arise from the abyss
of the past
into the mist
    of the future
    MESSAGES

    not of wailing
    & cringing
     & whimpering

messages
of the price of struggle
& the imminence of the inevitable

La Luta Continua

On the road to Blantyre
Zangaphee Chizeze

I
bare hills
and blue mountains
follow the road
on their haunches
while mango trees
adorn gentle slopes.

II
mountains loom
behind the showers
and the mist
like a nation's secret thoughts.
while bluegums stand
by the roadside
like soldiers on parade.

III
circles of hills
stand
like possessed dancers
riding the esctasy
of drums.

IV
little chibuku bars
cling to the road
while vacant groceries
gaze
like deaf mutes.

V
A lone hill
bears a gigantic wound
of rock
like a torn mouth
crying out in pain.

VI
and yonder,
the heavens
kiss
the earth.

VII
a crumbling hospital
of a colonial capital
stands
like an aged mourner
facing a state penitentiary.

Message to M One (1985)

Zangaphee Chizeze

tell the comrades
tell them that
out here
the burden
of enjoying freedom
daily
grows heavier and heavier
tell them that ...

Happiness
is like mist
upon a mountain;
it never stops for long
in any one place.

1985 : Action
Zangaphee Chizeze

gestures
of a tired continent
(devoid of emotion)
like a maiden's abandonment
of an unwanted child
in a pit latrine.

Question : 1985
Zangaphee Chizeze

could molotovs
really be the answer?

The New Covenant
(Dedicated to Dr. F.T.K. Sefe)
S.E. Chiziwa

Behind curtain, dapper smiles
A morning star heralds
The birth of a new tide
Thicker than the falling one
As a god rides on the crest of the wave.

The sun is up
Sing; The anniversary of our ascendancy
Cry! The anniversary of our impotence
For in climbing we stumbled
And the covenant broke.

The Dry Valley emits
Groans of deflated stomachs
blood curdling yelps
Guffaw of inflated bellies
All in the dale of cracking bones.

The Lord's strangling hand over Egypt
Calamity whistles in darkness
The living living lives
In the shadow of life
See! Shape-Changer's sadistic smile.

The Pilot snoring
Plane somersaulting
Primitivety reigning
Degeneration in creeping
Clock of Morality backward swinging.

Burning stars penpushing
This chapel, red in holiness
Repaint the chapel
No! Renew the covenant
Or winds of fate triumph.

Time heals the volcano's cough
Showers terrify mountains
Rivers cut their own valleys
Bathe in Bethsaida
And establish the new covenant.

Woman Speaking
Catherine Duclos

Why must I make you respect me?
Why must I alone carry the burden of giving life or death
Because of your swollen ego?
You make me accept this responsibility
As you carelessly spill you seed.
So what more can I do to make you trust me,
Besides spread my legs?
Oh, that's right,
You think all women have no conscience,
No feelings, no self respect, no intelligence, no morality, no love.
We aren't worthy of your trust?
We aren't worthy of your love?
Please, show me why,
Without sticking a needle in your eye.
The many of your mind are but the few I think.
Why then, can minority not rule?

Memoirs

Dunstan Gausi
(A retired soldier revisits the college).

Marching past in slow and quick time
the soldiers reminded him of emotions
Long since forgotten
The drum reminded him of bombs in Burma
But the parade itself, of home coming

When I looked at him
He reminded me of No. 12 Platoon
I thought of my platoon commander
Bald, old, irresolute, and seemingly defeated.
Two types of defeat

It gave me satisfaction to think
That his defeat was in age
True, it had defeated him
But the wealth of knowledge was rewarding

Tears erupted from the barriers
That bound my prestige
Inside, I saw and felt the searing pain
Of an entity retiring while its quality lasted

His retirement was just around the corner
His visions of further promotions were annulled
The world had suddenly turned vicious
And of all the 'old boys', fate had chosen only him

Suddenly the parade was over
The National Anthem started
We stood up at attention saluting mother Malawi
For leaving the force bald, old, irresolute, but alive:
The retired officer left the dais
Like the soldiers who had been parading
He was tired, and
Retired.

Operations and Tears
(In memory of a soldier whose wife mourned)
Dunstan Gausi

The tears coursed down her cheeks
Rebuking her projection
Shaming her
And rejoicing in their revealing powers

The tears collected at the base of her jaws
Fathering
Then mercilessly
Dropping off into the cloth that covered her breasts

The tears left a path of solitude behind
Her pale cheeks shone
Revealing the tears' course
And the misery that went with them.

She tried neither to sniff nor to wipe away
The remnants of a gouged personality
Out inside her heart bled
At the vileness of nature

The tears
The sorrow
The anguish
And the resignation
1980

A Woman's Cry
Cecilia Hasha

Sister,
If you happen to meet him
tell him that in matrimony
Hands are for caressing the wife's body
And fondling her breasts
Not a sjambok
for whipping her body
Or slapping her face.

Sister, sister
If you see the man
forget not to remind him
That a man's chest in bed
Is the woman's pillow
where she can pour her tears
In times of sorrow as well as joy
Not hardboard for manifesting his temper.

Sister, sister, please
If by chance you meet your brother-in-law
Whisper in his ears that in marriage
Lips are for kissing
And producing sweet nonsense
Thereby giving pleasure to each other
Not for kissing a calabash of beer
producing words fit for the bin thereafter.

Sister, sister, please, sister,
If you encounter the man I married
Remember to say to him that his eyes
Are there to admire his wife
The shape of her body
The beauty of her face
And the art of her hands
Not to lust after teenage girls.

Sister, sister, please, sister, Abiti Moya,
If you meet CHEJAFARI, my husband,
deliver to him this message:
Money in the home should be there
To maintain wife and young ones
Not to purchase risky pleasures
which he can have free and safe
from me, his wife, Abiti Daniel

Jaundice

Maxford Iphani

Even the air
which sliced through
My flesh,
Melted my bones,
Constructed a highway
Through my marrow,
And unbolted my whole,
Has utterly rejected me.
Now, it rushes
speeds by, past me.

My shadow does not go where I go,
It has chosen its own path.
My feet, too,
Do not point where I go.
My eyes do not see far off.

My freedom or
The vestiges thereof
Rules me with the hand
Of a commander of battalions.
I am free not to do this or not to do that
I am free to accept my fate and not to by-pass it
My smile has come to be
A distortion of my face
My voice, a muted grunt
Regulated by remote powers
Both visible and invisible;
Rendering my jaws locked.

My hopes, called such for convenience,
Have long degenerated into nothingness
In the massive holocaust of
What I dare to call the 'real' me
Because I think there is no 'me' any more
But the non-existent 'me'
Loathes with all might,
This lock-jaw status.

Masks
Maxford Iphani

Shifting from behind the small bush
With a mild stagger
He views the village again
This for the twentieth time
He has been in the bush two days now
He wants to return
To his hiding place
A thorn pricks him
In the right foot
He removes it and curses
He sits down at his place
Looks down, his head
Thrust between his two raised knees
Memories of the great day
Visit him again
They've been doing so so many times
He can't forget that day
He was dancer of the day
He had fooled everbody
He had fooled the elders
The Aphungu, the Anankungwi
Who were experts and specialists
In identifying stumps, pits or bitter cucumbers
What was most pleasant to him
Was the way women had behaved
The women had clapped hands for him
They had ululated for him
They had sung for him
And danced alongside him
He could see, they admired him
He had smiled to himself
And now he thanks the mask
For keeping that smile to himself
He had sent the drummers
Into a frenzy unheard of

The spectators were wild with excitement
Animals which danced like this were rare
They had seen only few
Women went crazy
At the lift of his right hand
Really mad at the way
He moved and shook his hips
Women went insane
To see how he leapt and landed on the ground
And they had clapped and clapped hands
And ululated and shed tears of admiration
But now he was here
Alone in the bush hiding
Forced to stay in hiding
By the same mask
That had triggered off
Massive jubilation in the spectators
He can't go home,
Not with that newly acquired face on him
Yesterday he tried twice or thrice
To go to the village
But everytime he approached
The nearest houses women and children
Ran away, scattered in all directions
For safety, even men raced for their huts
He gave up, and went back to his hiding place
His attempts today have all failed
Today the village was violent towards him
They set dogs on him
A stray animal is always feared
One never knows what it wants
He ran back fast
Who wants dogs to chase him?
He is now terribly hungry
He has not eaten for the last two days
It was impossible to eat
How could he?
The mask had stuck to his head.

It coudn't come off
It looked like a minor problem at first
But after several struggles with it
He realised the seriousness of his situation
He remembers the stories he was told
By his uncle years back
About the strange powers of Nyawu
If you put a piece of cloth to your head
In imitation of a Chadzunda
You might have it stuck on you
It has happened before, he had told him
And he makes another attempt
To remove the mask from his head
It is still part of him
It is as if he is trying
To tear his hair off his head
He cries quietly and tears ran down his cheeks
He thrusts his head between his knees again
Caresses his feather mask
The memories unfold again
Of the smiles of the women
The cheering of young been-to boys.
meanwhile the elders of the village
Are consulting about this strange animal
Which, of course, resembles the one
Which had danced so well the other day
There is also the issue of missing Mr. Zayekha
The eldest of them suggests
That they dispatch a team of young men
Armed with bows and arrows, spears, clubs etcetera
And accompanied by dogs that should
go looking for the animal
The team sets off
And heads in the direction of Zayekha's new residence.

* * *

He has fallen asleep
And is dreaming a painful dream
He has climbed a tree
He is nearing the top
When a look down
Brings a green snake in view.
It is approaching slowly
He senses it
He doesn't know what to do
He struggles with a branch
It doesn't break
He tries another, it doesn't
The snake is just about to bite him
When he wakes up with a start
He hears noises, twigs breaking
Soon he sees two young men
Flying at him, and shouting
Their arrows point at his chest
He wants to shout, identify himself.
But he can't, he is dumb
"Mr. Zayekha,
You've committed an unforgivable sin"
One of them shouts
He knows the young men
One of them is his own nephew
Two arrows are released, simultaneously
Darkness crowds on him, the pain fades
"He thought he could cheat the village"
One of the young men comments as
They lift the body of Zayekha
Off to where a pit has been dug by
Two other young men
As they lower him into the pit
Someone says pitifully, "You can't fool

your own society twice."
"Zayekha has been ejected," another one puts in
"He danced so well the other day,"
The team leader says "I still remember ·
The way the girls and women had
Rejoiced that afternoon"
The others shake their heads
And shrug their shoulders.

... Into the wilderness

Gustave Kaliwo

From every corner of the desert
East to west,
South to north
We all the same joys share
Silently mumbling
at this gift God has sent us.
It's a blessing
haven't you and me, all
heard it but for many a time repeated
we were oppressed so we prayed
for an able-bodied man
to take us out of Egypt.
Moses came,
silenced Pharaoh and his councillors
led us out into the wilderness
he alone and God knew where
he was taking us.
Do we dare ask?
Why?

He knows all,
he has God by his side,
and does counsel from him take,
how dare you ask,
Why this, this way should be?
Who in society is dangerous
he knows the punishment God desires for him
It's all for the benefit of the future
the future, of these our dumb children.

January, 1984.

The Uprooted
David Kerr

Our village was an easy walk from my
husband's grave; a path from the maize
plot cut past a baobab into the thicket
and I came each month to pour beer and seek
blessings; when the troubles grew worse
and salt was scarce and the banditos demanded
goats I'd walk deeper into the wood where
frogs were too frightened to croak,
and I scattered flour on my father's grave,
or deeper still where the creepers twisted
on grandfather's grave, where even grass-
hoppers were silent and the only sound
I could hear was the beat of my heart,
till blessings oozed from the ground,
and calmed me. But the banditos came
more often, snatching youths or girls;
they burned the school and beat those
too weak to stifle screams. All night
I spat out teeth and blood. I had to flee
with a bundle of clothes, spoons and plastic
cups on my head; Selina, wrapped tight
in calico, drummed her heels against my back;
gunfire boomed like funeral drums, smoke
stung our eyes - no time for last prayers
at the graves of men who'd left me.
We walked past forest, rivers, windswept
mountains till we reached the border in
the gloomy highlands. I kindled corn-cobs
for warmth, cradling Selina in my calico.
People here showed us hills for building
our shacks of grass and spattered mud.
Some men dug shallow latrines near our
huts which huddle the rocks for shelter.
Once a week smiling, uniformed white women
came in Landrovers to give us medicine for
coughs or malaria, plus a basket of flour

and beans; when I stagger to the stream
with my water pot, suckling Selina, tears
flow, not for the scabies on our skin or
the hard mat on dirt where we shiver all
night, but because I never had time to pour
my last flour and beer on the graves
in our home thicket, and all of us have
left fathers' graves in many villages.
Preachers roar all night in the camp
about Armageddon and the horned beast, saying
that even people here have quarrels,
and some have fled across distant borders;
the priests (who claim to know) say Satan
is uprooting the whole world and spirits
are howling around neglected graves like
these cold winds through stunted grass.

Starlight in Malawi
For Jack Mapanje. Free 10.5.91
David Kerr

The day the poet (after four
years in a window-less cell)
was released I drove him with
exultant chatter to his place
through a night of pale-straw
hills, and saying "I'd almost
forgotten how stars looked",
he leaned back as if to lick
them from his upturned face
on which torrents of starlight
fell.

Bare Truths
David Kerr

Here, where even village herbalists assemble
in jackets and ties, where tuxedoed demagogues
patch dreams with garish java-print wraps,
where the mouths of worshippers are gagged
by starched vestments, where the sick
and starving bury each other in shrouds
embroidered with developmental slogans,
where policemen polish non-conformist skulls
to a meticulous button-bright patina,
that mad girl, sprinting stark naked, knew
what she was doing, brandishing her clothes,
tied on a stick, at pedestrians, terrifying
cars with her feral eyes, before shimmering
through grass like a duiker into the forest.

Modern Auras from Chingwe's Hole
David Kerr

Chimombo has been here
like an eruption from down under
beneath charged tectonic plates
for a napolo
to end all napolos

Mapanje has been here too
with grain-throated ravens
scavenging for human carrion
extracted from this coily, ancient grave
pelting the bones on to his cell's roof
a whole hibernation at Mikuyu
spent in resigned vigilance

The precipice ever so steep
still hangs on the brim
of the vast void
looking so hazy now
obscuring the distant outline of Shire

The roots have grown moss
need peeling off to read
the strange old myths

The skulls
carried down the abyss
out of the tunnel
on to the jungle valley below
keep throwing up the aura
in their invisibility

Is it this voluminous dungeon
snaky in its endless journey
to the heart of Namitembo
that holds the wonder?

Is it the breath-taking view
hanging out from this cliff
infinite nothingness all around
superimposed
on the kingdom beneath?

The tricksters from Kasonga village below
pose as guides to unsuspecting tourists
while the numerous versions of myth
about Chingwe's hole
freeze into one chilly tale
of a dark night on Zomba plateau
where winter is perpetual
the scenery paradise
the atmosphere bliss
and forest fires, hell conflagrations.

Choices
Kapwepwe Khonje

After decades of development
Why are we still haunted by crocodiles
When we fought that beasts of prey
Should go with the dreaded colonialists

Why has the drought made us reel
With fits of devaluations and cat call strikes
When silos were full and reserves piling
and piling overseas?

Why these perpetual witch hunts
and the paralysis at frozen packages:
chanting these doomsday messages
of civil strife in variegated voices?

Haven't we moved thirty years
in a full circle

Haven't we been taught classics
at this transplant of Eton
where our skins don't qualify us
and local graduates are snubbed?

Haven't we argued in borrowed tongues:
dissecting the legends and ideals of
Napoleon, Shaka, Lincoln, Marx, Cicero
in the tradition of Whitehall

Haven't we?
Now, when coming to choices
Why shrink from foreign ideologies like vomit:
Aren't we reversing wheels of the history
we have been shaping all along?

Mother
Kapwepwe Khonje

The world grinds nerves:
I've been lonely in babbling crowds;
I've been trodden on my pauper feet
on the pavements;
And, I have retired to nowhere
A sleep-walker
as dreams dreamt die with years
clad in these patched patches;
carrier of gnawing hunger,
I still compete with dogs
at the garbage bins.
I've been through poisoned realities
But fattening on fantasies tires;
The city is not my home -
yet,
When I knocked at her reed door,
And she opened the fire warmth,
Her bony palm cold in mine, I
Masked the truth, the sad truth
That her son was a failure.
In her hut,
Sleep was polluted as foul smells
Crawled into the ecstasy of dreams
And her sorrow misted eyes
Saw the granary yawning;
I needed no words from her -
and,
Again at dawn's bird-songs
I crept out of her mud hut
Neither her curse nor her hand clap
Do I deserve in my wanderings
Dazed by the distant twinkling lights
and the city's sucker-power.

and,
Again I feebly wriggle to free her
From manacles of poverty, back
To pavements - a bowl of spite and
Sympathy I am casting hungry stares
Through shop windows,
and.
the rumbling stomach tempts;
it tempts the reluctant hand.

Limbo
Joji Ngoto Kummwenda

I open my eyes
To see
What do I see?
Dark
pregnant
clouds gathering.
I open my mouth
To speak
But I find teeth
Imprisoning my tongue

And straining .....
straining hard
to hear .....
I hear thunder ....
thunder rolling in the distance

Then .....
Lifting my feet
to walk
I am arrested
arrested in mid-stride

stones
lie
in my path
DEAD MUTE

Under the Tree
Monica Brenda Kumwenda

There my life ends
My whole being drowned
In a world of fantasy
Dreams come true
There my desires satisfied
My doubts cast aside
Yet my soul shaken to the core
The reality remains

Under the tree I say a little prayer
Counting the stars up
Numbering my days
Realisation that life is too short to live fully
Yet this life goes on
Hopes high, dreams piling up
I have to move on
Forge ahead

Under the tree
All my sorrows sink deep within
The shadow of death moves away
In thy presence
The urge to live on
Assurance of happiness
The long awaited happiness

Watching the world under the tree
I have to reach the peak
But success begins with the will
Awareness that the destiny has to be met
Intrinsic goals to be set
One step at a time … and life goes on
Beyond the sky's limits
My future displayed
Beneath the trading ground
We all are bound
Across the sea

And beyond the horizon
At the sunset
Lies a story untold
There a road to be followed

Under my hopeful tree
There are no fears
The world stops existing
yet life remains as cruel as always has been
Life remains so fateful
But under the tree
Trust life goes on.`

Unforgettable
Monica Brenda Kumwenda

Like a butterfly so free
Without barriers
No roadblocks
He came in disguise
Like a dove so peaceful
Like a deer so amazing
Like a child so innocent
Like an angel so protective
With a look in the eye issuing
Love, peace and harmony
One could never guess
What a cheat he was
I will never forget the unforgettable.

First chapter, it was so beautiful
So wonderful and enchanting
A wish upon a star
It would last
Final chapter, so indescribable
So tragic and heart-rending
The whole world would cry
Cry out words of sorrow
how so unforgettable it was.

A twinkle in the eye, a smile in the face
Happiness written all over
Tricked I was
Pricked I was, I would never forget the unforgettable.

And she, the innocent victim
Helpless like a child, so passive
Could only watch
So much for words, too much for the world
Terrible, horrible, treacherous it was all
A foul play so bitter and unforgettable.

Going to Sapitwa
Ken Lipenga

1
I hear no drumbeat here;
there's no chopa to be danced.
The singers have departed,
the drummers have gone to sleep,
and the moon weeps in mourning.
I break the past at crossroads
and depart for Sapitwa.

The last echo of an old dream
is blown away by the wind;
wounded masks bleed to death,
the wind whispers nostalgia
and the stars are embarrassed.
I break my pots at crossroads
and begin my journey to Sapitwa.

What, pray, is there to salvage?
Silence stalks the land
as cockroaches overrun the shrines.
Graveyard trees bend in shame.
The wise leave no footprints.
The gods have gone into hiding,
their shadows buried in rust.

Farewell, this valley of worms;
goodbye, artifice of convenience;
I go to rejoin the misty dance.
For me the waters of the beginning,
for me the fires of creation.
I carry my soul on my shoulder
and head for the heights of Sapitwa.

2

To Sapitwa is but a moment's turning
that brings together heaven and earth.
One magic flash of memory:
Suddenly the rocks are bedecked with song,
girded with calabashes of sweet poetry!
Yesterday is today, tomorrow is every day,
and history is but a wishful dream.

Kneeling before the Great Rock,
closing my eyes to all motion,
I shun the flow of the rivers,
turn my back to mortality,
stay dumb to all talk of decay.
I now return to the womb
to partake of the dew of innocence.

It takes only one arrow
to shoot down profane Time;
one bold leap into the abyss
to shake hands with a long-feared self.
All is unlearned, layers of lies peel
and fall to the ground:
Life breaks out as from a shell.

Upon Arrival at the Peak
Ken Lipenga

Alas! Others already here before me!

"This one has been here for sixty years;
this one traveled a thousand miles
to get here; this one arrived yesterday;
I myself was born here."

And so I'm condemned
to be a second-hand man,
mimic man in rags, mere shadow
of other people's shadows,
eternal follower,
repeater of obsolete deeds,
wearer of discarded clothes,
believer in hackneyed notions,
drinker of stale waters.

"And so you see
you are not the first to arrive here"

I'm not the first, I'm not the last.
My very song is a hollow echo
as I stand precariously in line
waiting for my turn.

I Salute the Wise, I Mourn the Future
Ken Lipenga

I stand to praise the wise of the land
before whom there was nothing,
after whom will be darkness and tears.

The future bodies ill for a slumber-drunk people.
On Sapitwa all looks well
when we forget we are only waiting.

We have been dreaming and postponing.
We threw wisdom to the winds
and hid behind ceremony and song.

We are late-comers.
This river upon which we sail
will not like the Shire enter the ocean
in the manner of an honoured guest.
The time for that is gone, my friend.
This river will fall
as from the heights of Sapitwa
into African reality,
and the waters that fly at landing
will be crimson and fierce.

And the wise will be gone then,
the wise will be long gone.
Only my children will be there to burn.

I stand to praise the wise of the land
before whom there was nothing,
after whom there will be nothing.

Midnight Pilgrimage
Ken Lipenga

Once a pool of restless waters
craving a return to innocence,
she burst out of the circle
one cold July morning it was,
and carved a silver path southwards
carrying tales of origins and schisms;
she would fashion fragments of dreams
into a bountiful linear vision
and ride on its crest to nirvana.
She cajoled mountains, bribed lakes,
valleys succumbed to her seduction;
she meandered past all obstacles,
she sped through towns and jungles;
she traversed the years undaunted,
she whose birth had begun with a rumour
freed from a blazing blasphemy.
In dry seasons she found shelter
under the canopy of friendly forests,
then dared the sun to a wrestling match.
In greener times her song of bliss
was heard far and wide, the very birds
paused to ponder upon her melodies!
She wrapped history in a slogan,
she tossed it at the dancing crowds
mingling with the reeds on her banks.
Delirious riverside dwellers, these were,
singing of the imminent millennium;
the hills echoed their chant
till the singers in orgiastic frenzy
pulled out their eyes, cut their ears,
fell prostrate, and in ecstasy
sought salvation under a shadow.
They refused to take food or advice
they pointed daggers at their hearts
they strangled their young ones
to teach them a lesson in obedience;

they buried themselves in the dust
they offered to drown themselves
in her waters for sheer gratitude.
She swept them along in her fiery path;
their songs died, but their voices
became her anthem: I am a nation,
says she, no longer a river;
look at my flag, my one-plane airline,
I am no more of the circle, I exist!
At times the lean voices of her poets,
lovers she had disdainfully abandoned,
did warn: proceed slowly, proceed gently,
respect the power of the seasons,
permit tributaries in your wanderings
lest the predatory torrents of this world
violate the purity of your cause.
But a fierce zeal can maim the eye,
a calm voice is no match for thunder,
a serpent's song vanquishes the ear
before an elder clears his throat to speak.
No one knows when the crash occurred--
the villagers still speak of two rivers,
one from the east, the other from the west.
Are Ruo and Zambezi the culprits perhaps?
But the villagers speak only in whispers.
We know only that the waters boiled,
and in the rising smoke was seen
the agony of heroes famous and unknown
all seeking apotheosis in the valley,
drenched in blood, the foatus of a millennium
was pulled out of a writhing present--
all this beneath the many-coloured arch
built from fragments of the broken circle.
Phantoms rose above the greenish-red waters
bearing begging bowls fashioned from fresh skulls,
and in the din of songs of the dawn
young river and old sea came face to face.
They clasped, they danced in a whirlpool,
a wild shriek, then all was silent.

Ascending Mt. Mulanje
Ken Lipenga

A dream will tell you
if you are meant to find her.
All you need you must carry
On your back: a spear,
a knife, a bag of flour,
an earthen cooking pot.
When at river Likhubula
You pause to rest, three paths
will spring forth, gateways
in the dark forest wall.
Take the first, and a flame
Will gush from the soil.
A second gate will also
catch fire from your foot.
The third will allow you
easy passage. One full day
you must travel on it,
till you stand beneath Mulanje,
a mountain black as life.
at this point a woman appears.
you dare climb my Mountain?
look, at its foot is a brook
With fish like drowning stars.
You will find a pool
beneath a tree exhaling fragrance.
Throw your goods in
and wash yourself." She it is
who owns the mountain,
fragrance-tree and pool.
Throw your pot into the water,
you will see it dive
Like an iron moon your knife and spear will dart
to its floor like thunderbolts.
Throw in your maize-flour
a fog of powder will spread
like a leprous milky way.

Only then should you plunge
and wash your filth away.
Go now to climb the hill.
If you slip on the cliff
you have more than you require.
Use one hand, one foot, one eye.
You will slide on slippery dreams.
Owls and feathers of eagles
will drift in harmony about you.
Look down to the mountain's foot,
with bluegum trees becoming
loose threads in a green robe.
Old river Likhubula runs
like a twinkling string.
When you see these, avoid elation!
If you avoid elation
you will reach a plain
with herds of strange beasts,
silver their hair, copper their horns.
You will see three villages:
Sun, moon, and morning star.
Approach the central village,
She whom you seek will come out.
You will tremble with fear,
but she will lead you by hand
into her house of many doors.
Listen carefully, say nothing.
She will pick worms out of your heart
and cleanse your profile with herbs.
Then, and only then,
Will you re-enter her womb.
Absorb what you can, and understand
that when you come out and down
you will retain nothing,
not a single extraordinary idea.
But you will be refreshed
as if you had drunk clear water.

The Second Harvest
(To our new government)
John Lwanda

Hope?
Should I dare?
This bitter sweet fleeting moment of freedom,
Snatched from tragedy by the barrel of a gun
Intoxicates me momentarily. Tantalising!

Hope?
Should I dare?
Cannot Leopards, like Chameleons,
Change their dirty black spots;
And free me from this mad carnival?

Hope?
Should I dare?
So our Gods became Men,
And promised a second coming!

Hope?
Should I dare?
Like the mother of five skeletal,
Drought starved, sunken eyed children;
Let me live to see the second harvest!

Winter Home Thoughts

John Lwanda

On a cold Glasgow day,
In among the smoky breaths and coughs
I am full of home thoughts
Home? Where is home?
Is it where the romantic heart is;
Or is it where the warm gas fire awaits,
As the wife worries and frets.

Home?
The fading memories of a romantic youth,
Pampered innocence and boarding schools,
Among the poverty and misery of my peers.
A land where the immortal one rules.

Home?
You are an exile in Babylon,
Swathed on cotton, worry and anxiety
Exiled and separated from your very roots
A shiftless, fearful alien living off his boots

Home?
Where is my home?
On this earth, do I have a physical home?
Pray, will I have a home spiritual in heaven?
Or is it all a deadly game political?

Home?
One day I will get home.
Without walking, worrying or running.
One day I will get home,
Without a passport, visa or waiting.
One day I will get home,
Without a language, song or dream.

Home?
The songs are the last reminders of home;
Bitter sweet music throbbing in my ear.
I have no need to be there physically for
I can hear the call from here!

Home?
Release me from this buzz under my hat.
My confusion does not know why or what,
If only this crazy bind I could unwind;
Sweet peace of mind would be my prize.
One day I will open the door,
And my home will be there as it was
Before: sweet harmonious and fair.

From Florrie Abraham Witness, December 1972

Jack Mapanje

There are times when their faith in gods
Really fascinates me. Take when the Anglican
Priest with all pomp and ceremony married
Abraham and Florrie, why didn't he realise
Abe and Florrie would eventually witness
The true Jehovah in his most pristine? And silly
Little Florrie, couldn't she foresee the run against
The only cards possible when she said her
'Yes, I do; for kids or for none?' And when
Florrie's mother dear, with all her Anglican
Limping love for her first and only daughter
Still intact, even when she thought she might
Still visit the prodigals notwithstanding, how
Couldn't she see that she too would be booted out
Landing carelessly bruised and in Mocambique!
The buggers! They surely deserve it;
They deserve such a good kick on their bottom.
I mean, there are times when their faith just
Fails me. Take today, when silly little Florrie
Should scribble a funny epistle on stupid roll-
And love did you have to call it thus? I mean,
It sounds so strangely imprudent of ... But ...
Anyway: Darling Brother, only God of Abraham
Knows how we escaped the petrol and matches
Yet we are all in good hands. They give us
Free flour, beans free and their kind of salted
Meat and fish. We've even built a ten-by-ten yard
Little hospital for our dear selves. Only we
Haven't got any soap. But we'll manage and do not
Be anxious over us here dear Brother; Mummie
And the kids are all in good shape. They send
Their Christmas greetings. Read well and, oh, note:
Psalms! Where in London is the blooming Bible?

Glory be to Chingwe's Hole

Jack Mapanje

Chingwe's Hole, you devoured the chief's prisoners
Once, easy villagers decked in leopard colours
Pounding down their energies and their sight.
You choked minstrel lovers with wild granadilla
Once, rolling under burning flamboyant trees.

Do you remember Frog the carver carving Ebony Beauty?
Do you remember Frog's pin on Ebony Beauty's head
That brought Ebony to life? And when the Chief
Heard of a beauty betrothed to Frog, whose dogs
Beat up the bushes to claim Ebony for the Chief?

Even when Fly alarmed Frog of the impending hounds
Who cracked Fly's bones? Chingwe's Hole, woodpeckers
Once poised for vermilion strawberries merely
Watched fellow squirrels bundled up in sacks
Alive as your jaws gnawed at their brittle bones.

Chingwe's Hole, how dare I praise you knowing whose
Marrow still flows in murky Namitembo River below you?
You strangled our details boasting your plush dishes,
Dare I glorify your rope and depth epitomizing horror?

Standing on Bunda Hill

Jack Mapanje

When her turtle scales peel
even the Chiefs must look away
lest the gods detain the rains
-they all fear here

Her mythical ears where Ngonis
choked fleeing Chewas once
reek of the teething days
of urchins smoking mice

Only the artist's version perhaps
a Berlings Kaunda bloodshot
Mother Bunda in concrete, grunting
within the walls of her own muck-

The House that Florrie Intended
Jack Mapanje

She was building a stone house here once
To match with the times, she carelessly declared
Selecting her slabs and passing them on to
Her husband to lay the foundation. Young
Abu and Jemu playing corkfloat beachball
Rolled on the fine dry sands of Koko Bay
Edi and Lizi washing their cassava to dry
In the hot sun, caught little fish in their
bamboo baskets stretching in joy and triumph
And on this tablet of rock I sat half-nude
I remember hatching a little revolution with
Myself, brooding on an arched life, my arms
Cupping the chin, the brow tensed, the legs
Crossed, watching the endless blue waters of
the vast lake curl, lap-lapping at my
Feet as little fish nibbled at my toes. Then
A loin-cloth fisherman, emerging from the men
Bent mending their broken nets under the shade
Of the lone beachtree, jumping into a canoe
Fettered to a nearby colony of reeds and grass
He sculled away lazily perhaps to check the night's
Fishtraps. Meanwhile, beyond those rocks that
Drill in birdshit like breasts in white bras
Or two eggshells, a sharp fisheagle lingering
Swooped down for his afternoon chambo. And
Florrie passed on the morning's last stone to
Abraham. What transpired after that, I cannot tell
Except that I dared briefly abroad and I gather
Florrie witnessed in protest; and I gather her
Radiogram, those rumba records the kids so much
Cherished, and the spring bed and matress, and
The fridge-the spoons and forks too witnessed her
Departure. And today when Florrie's kids stand
Desperate at my embarrassed door, I've come to see
The straggling cornerstones of her house intended.

On His Royal Blindness Paramount Chief Kwangala

Jack Mapanje

I admire the quixotic display of your paramountcy
How you brandish our ancestral shields and spears
Among your warriors dazzled by your loftiness
But I fear the way you spend your golden breath
Those impromptu, long-winded tirades of your might
In the heat, do they suit your brittle constitution?

I know I too must sing to such royal happiness
And I am not arguing. Wasn't I too tucked away in my
Loin-cloth infested by jiggers and fleas before
Your bright eminence showed up? How could I quibble
Over your having changed all that? How dare I when
We have scribbled our praises all over our graves?

Why should I quarrel when I too have known mask
Dancers making troubled journeys to the gold mines
On bare feet and bringing back fake European gadgets
The broken pipes, torn coats, crumpled bowler hats,
Dangling mirrors and rusty tincans to make their
Mask dancing strange? Didn't my brothers die there?

No, your grace, I am no alarmist nor banterer
I am only a child surprised how you broadly disparage

Me shocked by the tedium of your continuous palaver. I
Adore your majesty. But paramountcy is like a raindrop
On a vast sea. Why should we wait for the children to
Tell us about our toothless gums or our showing flies?

Making Our Clowns Martyrs
(or Returning Home Without Chauffeurs)
Jack Mapanje

We all know why you have come back home with no
National colours flanking your black mercedes benz.
The radio said the toilets in the banquet halls of
your dream have grown green creepers and cockroaches
Which won't flush, and the orders you once shouted
To the concubines so mute have now locked you in.
Hard luck my friend. But we all know what currents
Have stroked your temper. You come from a breed of
Toxic frogs croaking beside the smoking marshes of
River Shire, and the first words you breathed were
Snapped by the lethal mosquitoes of this morass.
We knew you would wade your way through the arena
Though we wondered how you had got chosen for the benz.
You should have been born up the hills, brother where
Lake waters swirl and tempers deepen with each season
Of the rains. There you'd see how the leopards of
Dedza hills comb the land or hedge before their assault.
But welcome back to the broken reed-fences, brother;
Welcome home to the poached reed-huts you left behind;
Welcome to these stunted pit-latrines where only
The pungent whiff of buzzing green flies gives way.
You will find your idle ducks still shuffle and fart
In large amounts. The black dog you left still sniffs
Distant recognition, lying, licking its leg-wounds. And
Should the relatives greet you with nervous curiosity
In the manner of masks carved in somebody's image,
There is always across the dusty road, your mad auntie.
She alone still thinks this new world is going shit.
She alone still cracks about why where whys are crimes.

No, Creon, There's no virtue in howling

Jack Mapanje

'It is no glory to kill and kill again.'
Teiresias, Antigone.

No, Creon, you overstate your image to your
People. No, there's no virtue in howling so,
How can you hope to repair Haemon, your
Own blood, our only hope for the throne,
By reproaching his body mangled by your
Decree and put to rest without the requiem
Or our master drums? What tangential sentries
Advise you to bemoan the dead by scoffing
Them publicly thus? Those accidents your
Flunkies master-stroked, those tortures &
Exiles fashioned, and the blood you loved
To hear, did we need more lies? Look now,
Even the village lads toss their coins for old
Creon's days. What cowardice, what perversity
Grates life-laden minds on our death-beds?

The Farms that Gobble the Land at Home
Jack Mapanje

The farms peacefully chew up the land at home
Bulldozing docile mudhuts, flattening broken
Reed shacks into neatly developed cakes, scattering
their goats, chickens, pigeons or mice in
The swirling sand which blinds the eyes at home.
One farmer gathers smaller farmers into WETs
(Wage-Earning-/Tenants) offering them thirty coins
Per day, stopping their mixed planting:cheap
Original ashes or compost manures are banned
(To maximize profits) and fertilizers (only farms
Can afford) imposed. Men no longer need the mines
For gold; even women become breadwinners (with
Specially planned female wages to ensure their
Domestic sweat is not impaired) on the land our
Fathers fought for us back home. Moonlight drums,
Fireside yarns are ripped under the auspices of
Rural Growth Centres & recreations (such as
Whoring) carefully instituted to breed foreign
Exchange (for our guns, droughts or videos). But
When it rains (kindly), the snails still drag
Along their shells, the frogs hop about their
Monotonous stalls; only they mustn't croak about
Their daily dregs or the pesticides which blacken
Their skins & corrode their lungs, lest huge blue
Or green caterpillars on patrol crush them. So, when
You walk about, only Peace & Calm Law & Order
Prevails on the fields that gobble the land at home.

Fears from Mikuyu Cells for our Loves

Jack Mapanje

Our neighbours' nerves behind those
Trimmed pine hedges of Chingwe's Hole
And the strategies they'll adopt when

They are approached by the Special
Branch, are familiar but horrify;
We rehearsed their betrayals weekly

'Where did you first meet, I mean,
What did he often boast about in bars;
When he played darts, what jokes?

Didn't he, in your considered view,
Behave in a manner prejudicial? So,
He bent even those straight lectures!

Did your children ever mix with his
And how often did your wife share
Home-ground maize flour with his?"

We recycled other fears and nauseam too
And what tricks to perform to thrive;
Only the victims' hour did we not know.

I recall, when our neighbur was
Taken eleven years ago, secret tears
On my wife's cheeks because visiting

His wife and kids or offering them
Our sweet potatoes in broad day was
A crime, her husband had just been

Invented 'rebel'; on the third day
University Office quickly issued her
Exit visa to her husband's village.

The feasts of our singular friends
We also reran: 'His detention was
Overdue, those poems! Don't mention

That name in my office; I hear he
Refused to apologize, how typical!
How is that woman and her kids still

Occupying that University house?
Those conferences he loved, it's us
Going now. Has he reached Mikuyu then?

We thought it was another joke!'
Today, I see your delicate laughter
And what abuse they'll hurl at you

Dear children, dear mother, my dear
Wife as your 'rebel' dad confronts
The wagtail shit of Mikuyu Prison:

'Shore up their brittle feet, Lord!'

The Delight of Aerial Signs of Release
(For Pat, David, Lan, Angus & Co)
Jack Mapanje

I
'And there, rebels will rot, rot, rot!'

II
Today, remembering the tyrant's boast,
I began to seek aerial signs of release
To take the brag on; then your thoughts
Warm, the bulletins, your precious verse
Burrowed in, rocking our walls of despair
And the jangling locks and keys; the boots
Today tensed to your honorary membership
Cards of International PEN (English
Centre and American Center), Rotterdam
Poetry International award, Fund for
Free Expression, New York, distinguished
Writers' demonstrations at 33 Crosvenor
St, London, Glasgow, Edinburgh, Toronto
And other adoptions: the Poetry Society
And Irina Trust, the BBC, Radio Deutsche
Vella, Radio Netherlands International,
Amnesty International, Africa Watch etc...
What spirit uplift, what hope repaired!
What parallels, what crushing solidarity!

III
Yet you say David Constantine's fine
Birthday lines to Irina Ratushinskaya
Encapsulate the frustration your feel
On your tough campaign for our release!
Of course, we have the verse in common
Also sweet exiles and gentle bravados
Against despots, so courage brethren;
You have combed enough of the beast's
Fleas to dispel the stench of our mire:

The head of detainees peeped in recently;
Mrs Thatcher was here, also the Pope;
The Moderator of Church of Scotland
Followed the Archbishop of Canterbury;
Even SADCC university ambassadors have
Been; do you realize the State House
Reply was forged? Your noble part is
Done; let the Gods take the arena now!

IV
Exempli gratia, only last Friday
Thousands of dragon-flies swarmed
Over our prison yard like hungry
Locusts brooding over tender green
Shoots; we held tight the memories
That keep these sagging souls alive
As *nyapala* Disi dispersed our fears:
This spectacle you see above has
Been here once in the fourteen years
Of my trial; two hundred political
Prisoners walked out of these gates
Free, reducing the seven hundred
And eighty-eight stinking breaths
That crammed these dark chambers!
He pointed to Allah above in glee.
And today, as the damp Mikuyu walls

V
Begin to lichen, hundreds of moths
(Ostentatiously spotted in gold on
Black, green on pink, white on purple,
What not) land on this rusting wire-
gauze; but before I feel my pulse,
Disi brings me more from the walls
To fondle, he says; since I defend
Even the rats that nibble at those
Rare home-brought avocados or these

117

Lethal mosquitoes, why don't I count
The spots of these moths to see how
Allah kindly brightens our abattoirs?
And I surprise myself how quickly I
Chorus Disi's: This spectacle too
Has happened once in this fourteen
Years ordeal here and more political
Prisoners will soon march past these
Stubborn gates of Mikuyu...Christ,
These airy signs are thrill to seek!

The Deluge of our Gweru Prison Dreams
Jack Mapanje

(After the 1992 Chirunga and Kabula riots by students and workers: a
history of the nation, for David Rubadiri)

I
Today, the HM Prison Gweru dreams that
Fogged our vision once began to rupture

One by one: that pride of Capital Hill
Splintered in the heat of our endless

Droughts, the fallout muzzling the most
Civil of tenants; his luminous great

Lakeshore highway is crustaceous tarmac
In broken china, with yawning potholes

That crack landrover absorbers worse
Than those forest dirt roads long ago;

Even our quiet University students (having
Carefully balanced the shards of the beast's

Fantasies) only recently dared to sue
The Chairman of University Council for

Embezzling the truth and our University's
Head of Law for once defended justice!

After that happy debris of the Berlin Wall
And the Donor Community's 'good riddance',

Which piqued goat won't feverishly nurse
His tics, stunned by the inexplicable

Directions of these anti-despot missiles?
And however often he might violently

Kick about the pact he made with the devil
Three decades ago when you abandoned his

Kraal, I will dine with the devil himself
To centralize my Gweru dreams, he revved;

Yet after our Nelson Mandela's release,
Even the devil's generosity must tire.

III
When battered hyenas fail to crack
Rotten bones in the dustbins of East

Versus West, the time has come for our
Youths to dance; and let them take

The arena; what phantom model would
Not shed her varnish and cower under

The strain of time and despot desires?
Those fatigued Ndirande varicose veins

Were bound to burst on to the streets
Of Kabula. And what scapegoats will

Be imagined, what rebels lurking on
Borders invented! But there was no

Masauko Chipembere, no Jomo Chikwakwa
This time to spur on these Ndirande

Grassroots beyond the fury of those
Rhinoceros horns of your Clocktower

Riots long ago; and let nobody load
It on Dunduzu or Yatuta Chisiza; there

Was no Silombera, no Kanada to publicly
Hang here; as for Aaron Gadama, Dick

Matenje, Twaibu Sangala, David Chiwanga...
They shamelessly accidentalized these.

IV
Yet the children are entitled to wonder
How we allowed it, how such Gweru prison

Vagaries, without true mystery without
Depth deluded us worse than our gods.

Indeed, who's never had prison dreams?
You must have locked up your own dreams

At HM Prison Khami, Bulawayo in 1959.
If wagtails at Mikuyu Prison only months

Ago dreamt their lizards and even I dreamt
Tearing up lions, hounds and leopards

Which in defeat served scones and tea
On bamboo trays to my released inmates,

If I fought gaseous reptiles, sometimes
Waking up the whole cell at midnight,

Shouting and heavily breathing-what,
Who's never had dreams in these daily

Prisons? But as the inmates at Mikuyu
Said afterwards, Not even our nyapala's

Deliria in D4 (and the bloody prefect's
Here without charge sixteen years) could

Dig anybody's pittance of pit latrine
With his Mikuyu dreams, let alone build

A nation! Whatever, the question still
Lingers: won't toxic mushrooms burgeon

Under those rotten logs of nightmares
That now threated apres moi, le deluge?

Dried Bones, Steel, and Sirens
(for honourable Wiseman and Nthaziyake who claim to understand why)
Zeleza Manda

Even I,
standing at Sapitwa
trying to peer into Chingwe's Hole
in search of answers
to our daily "why?",
Can still see
between God's two giant pillars
green shrouded black cockroaches
bloodsucked and scourged
as they search for life in dustbins
probably to save enough for
their minimal annual rents.

damn it!'
Even I,
can still see
the messiah in chains
and a crown of thorns
led to Golgotha-the valley of
dried bones
cold steel
and sirens.
To Golgotha is dragged
he who championed us
against the midnight World of
Pharisees and Saducees
into dawn.

'Damn it!'
shall I then leap from here
and be halle-lujahly jesussed, too,
to salvage them,
damned cockroaches
and this messiah whimpering
in pains
of chains
or just await
time's decision?

Note: Theme: strictly religious
       Personae: certainly Jews
       Time: Probably all seasons
       Place: Doubtfully heaven.

Whispers
Alfred Matiki

My ancestors too
have been to the mountain top
from Kambiri Point
they saw him
stand sentinel over
embryonic poets
scavenging the remains
of poetic inspiration

They too
saw him fall into
the yawning abyss,
but tell it in broken
whispers of the dead dawn,
and mine the mute
in the shifting sands
of the day.

The thump and tremors,
felt in Gordon and Red Squares
paralysed the subterranean serpent
to frantic gesticulations
and impotence,
still strum the haunting tune
or question marks.

Was the fall
nature's making or
human design?
Wasn't he circumcised before?
Didn't he dance *chopa*
to need the foxtrot?
Didn't he immunise his lines too,
from mythical rhapsodies,
to remain sacrosanct
and guard the changing
colours of chameleons?

My ancestors know too
that the little ones still salivate
on his pickled metaphors,
modelling, traversing
the sand dunes of creativity,
tossing about the time bomb,
unsure to survive the censor's noose.

The Road to Emmaus
(for Easter)
Zondiwe Mbano

On this winding road
A shadow is close by me

On this lonesome road
a shadow trails after me

Extending from my heels
East to the sun's cradle

And now the sun is setting
Slowly into lurid clouds

Spread behind the ridge
That sends out darkness

A shadow is close by me
On this wandering road

Yet darkness attracts me
As flames attract a moth

Oh my Lord, draw nigh
On this road to Emmaus

Princes
Zondiwe Mbano

Amakhosi balibele nokudhla
Abayazi oluzayo

Princes are engrossed

In feasting
They do not notice
Their tower crumbling

Men are engrossed
In wrangling
They do not notice
Spears glaring

Women are engrossed
In gossiping
They do not notice
The baby crying

Boys are engrossed
In titivating
They do not notice
Their relish charring

Grey heads are engrossed
In story-telling
They do not notice
Their sun setting

Why, Oh why?

Zondiwe Mbano

Daughters of Lukonkobe
Dressed up in colours of flowers
To meet a blind suitor;
daughters of Lukonkobe
Why, oh why

Mothers of Lukonkobe
Elected an impotent slave
To marry the chief's daughter.
Mothers of Lukonkobe
Why, oh why

Sons of Lukonkobe
Whistled and chanted praises
To embolden a craven bull.
Sons of Lukonkobe
Why, oh why

Men of Lukonkobe
Danced the victorious *mgubo*
 To welcome a famished runaway.
Men of Lukonkobe
Why, oh why

Elders of Lukonkobe,
When a he-goat is mad,
Don't you knock off its horns?
Elders of Lukonkobe
Why, oh why

Viphya
(Ooo Viphya, Viphya wabazungu)
Zondiwe Mbano

Ooo Viphya
Viphya of the whiteman

Welcomed *machona*
From the bowels of gold
To bury them in the lake

Ooo Viphya
Levelling iron
Over the waves

Viphya of the whiteman
Mass iron coffin
Deep under the lake

Beware, Millipede
Zondiwe Mbano

Now that the *msangu* tree
Is bringing forth leaves
adieu rain, adieu visitor

Now that birds twitter, building
Nests up in the *msangu*
Beware millipede, beware fool

From mountains, rivers run
East through dry lands
For waters must hasten to the lake

From above, the sun stares harsh
Over lands scorched brown
And wildfires lick the land to ash

Adieu rain, adieu visitor
You flood rivers and lakes
But fail to fill holes of ant-hills

Now that the *msangu* towers
In greenery, with nests
Dangling like succulent fruit

Beware fool, beware of the heat
For under the *msangu* are thorns
And the baobab gives no shade

Beware, for October is a furnace
Melting and casting to rings
The metallic glow of your segments

Beware millipede, do not burrow
For bulldozers lift the earth
And grit it between their teeth

Martyrs
Zondiwe Mbano

Pakupoka wanangwa
Pali suzgo na wiphyo
Vitanda vikugona
Madindi ghakuzura

Songs on the radio
Raise our hearts high
To the praise of martyrs

The word of the preacher
Reminds us of our debt
To those who died for freedom

Martyrs are everywhere
In Uganda, Afghanistan, Zimbabwe
South Africa, Chiradzulu, Nkhata Bay...

But are they also martyrs
Who died for an unknown cause
That shall never be realised?

* * *

Chilembwe fumes at *thangata*
Chilembwe pounces on Listonya
Chilembwe slays Listonya

A furious mob rushes at the Dona
The mob knock down the Dona
And cut *mphini* on the white thighs

Chilembwe rescues the Dona
Chilembwe sets her on a horse
The horse gallops to Limbe

Gallops straight into the train
Gallops to Salisbury, Cape Town
Gallops home to Great Britain

Guns rumble over Chiradzulu
But Chilembwe is inside the bell
And later gallops to America

* * *

Mumba organised the N.A.C.
Mumba phoned the white Queen
Mumba was invited to London

And the natives threw a tea-party
To bid bim successful voyage
But they put poison in his tea

At Cidikalala women and men
Gathered to see the Madang'ombe
And bid him *paweme* to London

Children danced round the van
Puffing slowly into the village
But they did not see the Madang'ombe

And when the van was opened
They saw a shiny boat-like box
To ferry him on the voyage across

* * *

Joni will come again
In the flashing of lightning
Furious against *thangata*

These belching estate owners
With fleets of lorries and trailers
Ferrying tobacco to the auction

Batten on unshod tenants
With shorts strung precariously
To their scrawny waists

When Chilembwe comes again
And Levi Mumba of Lukonkobe
What song shall we sing to them

* * *

Our villages that reared martyrs
Have become ruins where rats
Deride the very idea of martyrdom

And sons and daughters of the craven
Have snatched the hunter's portion
Listen to their deafening song and drum

Sure we are tough-skinned people
Baked in the kiln of hardships
And our backs trained in stooping

But how long shall a hunting-dog
Relish chewing a clean bone
when cocroaches fatten on meat

Jacked up (To Golgotha)
Rowland Mbvundula

No quakes thundered that solemn dawn.
In disapproval earth refused to respond
When they wrenched us
of our one and only.
Fire and brimstone stood obliviously aloof
When he was whipped off
to the harsh heights of bony calvary.

The Iscariot soul mongers
Who traded in his (priceless) flesh and bone
analysed and kissed
his vociferous lips to fractured silence,
Jacked the unsuspecting victim
to protesting calvary.

Desperate eyeballs implored
cried in earnest plea
that his day commence not with peril.
But sirens screamed him off his noble stool.
Deep blue lightning flashed him away so soon.
Heavy arms weighted his upwilling spirit
with the enormity of a massive cross,
underpricing the invaluable alloy
As they took ascent to blood crucifixion.

In this Hole
(In memory of John Bandawe, 1939)
M. Mkandawire

Now that I am here
I look behind
And wonder.

Where are those soldiers
Who led me here
Into this dark hole?

Those who came to blow out
The evershining candle from my home
Where are they?

I can remember
How painful it was
When I crawled into this hole.

I cried with pain
Like the day of my circumcision
Nonetheless, I crawled into the hole.

This hole is dark and deep
Below the scorching and sticking soil
And leading to nowhere.

Where is that white collared man,
Who convinced people to pray to the white ancestor
And uprooted the people

The man who preached
Of river of salvation.
And reunion with old friends.

Where are those who preceded me?
Where is the river of salvation
I need salvation and reunion.

Why don't I go again?
Again to the green pastures
And tell them the truth.

Alas! Who am I
If not a naked spirit
Stranded in this strange hole.

The Dance
Felix Munthali

I dreamt of vipers
caged in a ring of fire
while men and women
prepared for a dance.
The end had come.

We have waited for this dance
since the news of dawn:
our sight is blurred
and our feet are aching-

the vipers of today
flourished as well
in the jungles of yesterday
soiling our rites of passage
and the grooves of history,
scarecrows to a youth
frittered on dreams

Dreams won't do
and baptism by fire
awaits holy innocents
butchered by jealous kings
who die in their beds
unaware of the cry heard in Rama
Rachel mourning her sons
because they are not.

I draw a rainbow
across the mists of my day dreams
for in the next rehearsal for the dance
neither the floods of bloated opinion
nor the numbness of bars of steel
shall have dominion over me.

Lines written from Chileka Airport, January, 1979.
for Peter Chiwona, Peter Mwanza and other friends
Felix Munthali

It won't do, either, will it?
It won't do
to look on us as protean
neo-mythical spirits
with a disappearing act
and a resurrection showpiece:

We exist in flesh and bones
though we have not ruled out
the intervention of miracles
in the affairs of men.

for sometimes, I fear,
we do more than merely exist:
we live-

how else would you explain
that descent into hell
with all its paraphernalia
of a bad funeral:
unpaid bills, repossessed cars
premature widows
children shocked out of their infancy
friends and colleagues
snarling at our memory and
some, we are told,
gathering for a game of bawo
and crates of beer?

Then if waiting be a taste of limbo
we have had that, too
nursed by the cheers
and tears
of friends and family
and now this

the metamorphosis
then next to gargantuan wings
and blinding light:
metallic and electronic
paraphernalia
of a modern resurrection!

When you are airborne
to Addis Ababa, Paris or London
on matters of international concern
let not those tattered blankets
and that clammy cement floor in Hades
overshadow your memories
or distract you from the gist
of your papers-
"Inter-Agency" meetings
are greater
than any of us

and in times like these, brothers,
let nothing overwhelm you:
all change is a whirlwind
though, in a way,
all change is expected.

They no longer grate on our ears
these unfamiliar names in exotic places;
our eyes no longer blink
at unusual faces
in flag-bedecked limousines

Why groan at the numbness of spirit
and the void in our minds
in times like these?

Imitate the fairies
whom men think you are:
study the freshness of the breeze
on Sapitwa;

survey the Shire from the top of Zomba Mountain
and guard against being swept
through Chigwe's Hole
into Namitembo River
the river of the dead,
the Styx of our ancestors

and perhaps on a bright day
have a look at the hot springs of Machinga
and the sandy beaches of Mangochi

for sometimes, I fear
we need to go beyond existence:
we need
to live

The Reply from the City
(for Jack Mapanje)
Felix Munthali

From us to you, dear Sisters,
sad, very sad, that one
about your still living on bonongwe
and still exposing your you know what

To hear you sing
and recite our creed
one would think
the millennium had come

We on our part
have been taking in our strides
wars and rumours of war
Ayatollahs, Shahs, Idi Amins,
detentions and aftermaths of detentions,
these catarrhs and measles
in the winds of change

To quote the poet
'we have been living and partly living'
trying to see the silhouette
behind our blurred vision
of the beauty of dawn

We have heard the news
but we need time
to follow your footsteps
to this land
where rivers flow
not with the clear water of Mulunguzi
but with milk and honey.

Wind of Change
Felix Munthali

Tantalising, isn't it, tantalising
the vision of a world without codes,
with no doors bolted
before you can begin to vomit
the accumulated bilge
of a decade without air

A butterfly flits across my path
without fear or favour
like that bird on the *mlombwa* tree-
we never think of Ham or Cain
or some such scapegoat
of our bestiality to man
to explain its yellow spots on a black body

I dream of open spaces
and voices circling the globe
with no bugs attached.

Did Harold MacMillan
mean that too
or was he only thinking
of other changes?

Neocolonialism
Felix Munthali

Above all, define standards
prescribe values
set limits: impose boundaries

and even if you had no satellites
in space
and no weapons of any value
you will rule the world

Whatever tune you sing
they will dance
whatever bilge you spill
they will lick
and you may well pick
and choose
their rare minerals
and their rich forests

They will come to you
in fear and trembling
for the game will be played
according to your rules
and therefore the game will be played
only when
you can win

Above all,
prescribe values
and define standards
and then sit back
to allow the third world
to fall into your lap.

Symbiosis at Chejusu
Felix Munthali

Some would say
that here was nature's dream world
with sparrows, linnets, cuckoos
cooing from the tips of sunless groves
zooming in like jet-fighters
at an air-show
to nibble the trimmed lawns
of secluded villas
where petals are blown in
from man-made forests
like manna to the children of Israel

Our children swore
they heard the voice of a leopard
and a thud-thud-thud
coming up our yard
and Luso our youngest daughter
swears she saw the leopard scratching our doors
asking to be admitted!
But suppose the doors had been open?

II

When shadows fall
the lyrics of birds give way
to the chant of owls and the howl of hyenas,
the plains and valley to the east of us
become a dark ocean covered by a storm-cloud
while that gigantic majesty
to the west
becomes a tilted wave
threatening to engulf us

We must wait for dawn
we must wait for the sun
to return to our Eden:

this symbiosis, a terrible beauty,
is also deadly.

III

In times like these
at an hour like this
when I trudge from Malemia Hospital
to No. 1 Forestry Road
it is neither the thunder of the waterfall

below the bridge
nor that pitch-dark confusion
in the grove around the corner
that one needs to fear
(it is only a tuft of a rainforest!)

No, the fangs of death
do not lurk in such corners:
the leopard howling in his grove,
the monkey leaping for safety
the snake sliding into the womb of the earth

these have their appointed hour
coming and going
in the fulness of time
seeking at the ticking of the clock
only what they really need.

What man needs to fear
in times like these
is the olive branch
extended out of convenience
and out of convenience
hoarded on a dung-hill

the meaningless smile
replied by a grimace,
the mechanical salute

acknowledged in anger and contempt

True enough
at an hour like this
empty spaces are filled by fear
and the sky itself
becomes the storm surrounding our earth
and yet I say,
not these
not nature in all its negative fury
can equal
the forest of man's heart.

Kavuluvulu

Felix Munthali

Was ever a defiance more complete
than that a man rise and fly
out of 'maximum security'
neither in the hailstorm of gangsters' bullets
nor in the creaking cacophony of a helicopter
but in the soundless chariot of a whirlwind?

Leaves rebelling against trees
particles of dust seceding from the earth
grains of sand defying gravity
escort him
like angels the risen Christ
into the timeless vistas of freedom

No, not for him
not for him the labours of Sisyphus
the rocks that turn men into rocks
youthful heads greying before their time
to wither away in silence and despair

Kavuluvulu was seen
to charter the elements themselves
to fly him
to a destiny of his choice.

No use talking of prison lore
or even black magic -
far too many have rotted
who were household names
in the land of the living
while Kavuluvulu carries on
running errands
to which only the free can go

We saw him command prisoners
distribute fish, rice and sugar

control the prison economy
as if nothing could touch him

He had come and gone
several times over
but for his dare devilry
his legendary kindness
his cool movements
he has more than earned his name
Kavuluvulu, the whirlwind.

Look Back in Shame

Felix Munthali

Things will get worse
before they get better
Our third of the tripartite globe
spins on its misery
not all of it of our own making
no doubt,
but we must stoop and wash
in the blood of innocents
executed at dawn
we must lie down and share
the clammy numbness of the floors
to which men are condemned
without charges and therefore
without trial

The stench of rotting bodies
fouls the air in Kampala
Amin's soldiers on departure
leave only bullet-holes
in the starved bodies of innocent men

and from Vietnam
men entrust themselves to the high seas
rather than bear the racism
of a people
who fought a gruelling war
to dislodge racism

in the impotent corridors
of sweet diplomacy
you can hear men talk
of an 'ideological vacuum'
and 'inter-tribal warfare'
they talk of things
and not of men

Look back in shame, look back
to the Pan African Congress of 1948
to the Bandung Conference
on Afro-Asian solidarity;
look back in shame
to the rainbow of dawn
now lost in the garish haze
of coups, counter-coups
and endless detentions

Black stands for the people:
green is the beauty of their land:
red is the blood we spill
to regain the land -
but what have we gained
'with carrion men
groaning for burial?'

We wake up wondering
into what insects
we are going to be changed
and the corrugated joy of our lives
has now been mangled
beyond recognition

Of course, we had wanted the land
as it was
with hopes and loyalties
firmly glued
to the beauty of dawn
where little lambs would frisk
in the summer of their prime
and lions would fret and growl
in the seamless cage of the rule of law

no, not this sunless desert
where carrion men
groan for burial.

Iran, 1979
Felix Munthali

Hurrah!
I say, 'Hurrah!'
to those horrendous hordes
storming the walls of privilege everywhere

It takes less, doesn't it?
ridiculously less, at times, it seems,
than the fire-power of the Shah of Iran
to look class, race and tribe
in the face and shout
'No more!'

It takes less
and yet it is probably more
than the ecstasy of revenge
or the rainbow
of what might have been
and may yet be

and the remote inspiration
of a religious leader
in the suburbs of a foreign city
seems too meagre, somehow,
too fantastical to bring
these awakened millions to the streets

the spirit of man
has been sanctified
by rivers of blood
and lifeless bodies
gassed to insanity or death-
entrails fall out of men who cry
'Freedom', 'Kwacha', 'Uhuru'

II
Airborne by earth-shaking whirlwind
it pays to speak in riddles
so that marooned on a precipice
by one of your doctrines
you can switch on
anyone of your thousand and one meanings
which the people of Iran
may perhaps have forgotten -
who has ever won a battle
against an oracle?

Better speak in riddles
lest the price you are exacting
on Iranian freedom
be seen for what it is:
blood-thirsty chicanery and
sanctimonious cant.

Better speak in riddles
lest the anodyne you are prescribing
turn out to be what it is:
sticks and lumps of clay
in the bag of a charlatan

You had better speak in riddles
for the agonies of dawn
are altogether too real
for the rainbow
in your mind

Waiting for the Rain
Felix Munthali

Blank faces smile and nod
above limp hands
clapping their automatic
soundless and unintended
welcome
It has been done, before, done
under every shade and colour of sky
from overcast, dark red to very clear

The robust and sweating poor of our sort
clap hands, sing and ululate
for Land and Range-rovers
Mercedes Benzes and Toyota Crowns
Six-O-Fours and Datsun B's
forerunners of forerunners
with multi-coloured flashlights
and whizzing sirens
on their rooftops

It's been done, before, done
this ululation of the dispossessed
for the tired smile
and the tired nod
tired and sad
from praying for the rain

The poor and sweating of our sort
have been here since dawn
clapping their hands
for every moth that frets and shouts
its hour upon the stage
blinking at the multicolored lights
and wailing sirens
taking them
into the land of milk and honey

Lines Written after Reading Ngugi wa Thiong'o's Petals of Blood
Felix Munthali

No, no monuments yet
to Dedan Kimathi
and all the champions
of our struggle for dawn, none!

Has it sometimes seemed to you
that this is as it should be?
That we would be spitting
on their sacred memory
by erecting them monuments
in times like these?

Monuments should breathe
the ambrosia of victory
of the war that might have been won
even if a battle or two
had been lost.

Those indomitable spirits
of our tropical rain-forests
are rarely evoked these days
except, perhaps, in cynical sanctimonious mockery
by sleek money-winged smoothies
who turn initiation songs
into the mindless howl
of cocktail circuits

who will use sacred oaths
to defend
their primary
secondary
tertiary
and perpetual
accumulation

No, no monuments yet
while babies in Zimbabwe
are blown to pieces
as 'collaborators'
no, not while the Mandelas and the Sisulus
are still breaking useless stones
on Robben Island
are being turned into stone
by men without entrails

Leave it to the manipulators
to force themselves on newspapers
and on the perplexed
and contemptuous faces
of the people

Our real heroes are better left alone
alone in the minds of the young
in the wilderness of Majengo
to ferment in darkness
like a grain of wheat!

In our Part of Town

Felix Munthali

Riches in our part of the town
are not to be seen
in twins or triplets
or even quadruplets of cars
lounging around split-level homes
as is often the case in North America
but in the parallel societies
promenading the by-ways
at the approach of dusk.

For every human wish, foible
a menial is on stand-by
from the day men are born
to the day they fly home
or fall from grace.

Among one set of dependents
children run around on tricycles
or play with models of electric trains;
sometimes build hangars
for their jet-planes
and fighter-bombers
while in the other set of dependents
children bend wires and carve stalks of maize
to build their VC10's and Concordes;
they mould seven-ton lorries
motor cycles and Ilalas
marooned in smoky verandas

Indeed, but for the grace
of our colonial past
and the ogre of poverty
wives who would have been
doing their own laundry

or pounding their own maize
are clutching escapist pulp
and dreaming of Gymkhana Club
or Apollo Cinema

And when the shame of it all
parades before us
we run for cover
behind a fig leaf called ologies and - isms
and speak of a 'labour intensive society
on the verge of economic take-off'

bored and elegant housewives
lead loaded processions.
out of the market
and supermarkets
to be swarmed by urchins
peddling
sad - looking carvings

Which way
is this take-off,
I wonder?

An African Tragedy
Bright Molande

The long flight of the soul from Heathrow came to an end.
The home landing was well patronised and supervised,
Even a daughter born in my absence was here
To relieve the stranger of the boon of ear dogged books
But it was my uncle who really plunged me home.

Son, the grave is an insatiable stomach, it only swallows,
He said and drifted on with the wind that has been sweeping home.
    Since the day you left the village, we've been

```
                              falling
                        g e n t l y
            spinning
flopping        p
                i
                   n
                    n
falling                 i
   gently                 n
      one by one           g
          like              in
          lonesome leaves       the wind,

              in the wind of death
         down

              to bottomless graves.
```

We drove home, parked and walked the old footpaths of the village
Then came the ritual of a son once lost in distant lands:
        visiting African village graves.
Here gathered all lunatics, heroes, villains, clowns and martyrs of the land.

John Chilembwe knelt on a ragged rock, praying.
Kamuzu quietly squatted before a calabash,
        Washing hands in steaming blood.

Mandela sat leaning against a tree in the back shadows, worriedly
        Listening to the distant roaring of thunder and whispers of death
As Mugabe perched on a jagged tree stump, mauling raw flesh.
After offering their bones, blood, beer and flour at the door of the shrine
Muluzi and Mkape jumped into a drunken dance of the gods
Revelling and gyrating to the rain dance of rock'n'roll
Pleading with ancestral mothers for this African Tragedy.

And the was a gentle knock from within!
Salvation must be at the foot of the door!
There are voices from under the door of the Labour ward.
But ha-aah, it must've been a knock of the wind
For this is all I can hear from the delivery cave:
        Groaning
Gasping for air,
        Whispered fears
Sighs
        Whispers
Whispered sighs
        Suddenly-

        Silence!
Furious silence!

I am sick inside me, my inside is sick
As Africa keeps delivering astride hungry yawning graves.

The Child Chilungamo Will Be Born
Francis Moto

I had told you in whispered tones
that fate had twisted our thoughts
Had I not told you that one day
we would dance a poetic dance
twice removed from time?

I told you that the hand of fate
had carved our history
on the sands of burning shame.
A people's reasoning taken prisoner
sang songs about
the coming of the other dawn.

As the clouds coiled round the hills over the lake
we made love on the pebbles of the beach
watched by the open blue sky above.
Echoes of songs from the mountains
in the west met with the songs
sung by birds in the hills over the lake.

Then our thoughts wrestled
with the mysterious forces
that had arrested creativity
in its youthful tracks.
A fearful unseen voice
threatened our very existence.
Men wearing secret clothes
followed our shadows to the sacred hills.
Where were the flames that once lit this land?
We needed flames to eat away
the shadows of darkness.

By the hills we plucked sweet red berries
and rode a whirlwind on our way down.
Our tongues coiling around the fresh juice,
we sang ancient songs

in praise of the path of light.
And on the roadside we picked
the first pumpkin of the season.

Again we made love on the pebbles of the beach
watched by waves gently approaching the shore.
Do you remember the sharp blade of grass
that cut your soft flesh?

Soon the boy Chilungamo will be born.
I told you as we sipped our glasses
of an imagined new dance
to calm my nerves which had been stretched
to their limits.

Now you will tell me, mother of Chilungamo,
that your days are due.
My heart is working extra hard
as it waits for the news
of the coming of the boy Chilungamo
or will it be the girl Chilungamo?
For what does it matter, a boy or girl?
Chilungamo will still be the child's name.

We have been through some delicate days
of weighing and balancing on the scale of survival.
Questions we have been asked:

How do you people manage
to say nothing?
Do you mean you cannot speak at all?
And even you educated ones,
you mean after all the books
you have read you cannot raise a finger
and say something about anything?

a voice from the land of spirits would intervene:

They speak a language
only they can understand.
In silence they have learned
to speak with eyes.
In silence they have learned
to speak using a language
selected by the experts
of silent communication.
Some day you will come to learn
that they were speaking all along.

Silence, our friends, was an art learned
for the sake of simply wanting to be there
and I can assure you, mother of Chilungamo,
I cannot wait to listen to the first cry
of the child Chilungamo.
And I cannot wait to set my eyes upon
the little soft feet and feel the soft skin.
And I hope I will still be there
when the child takes its first steps
of cyclic motion.

I still remember the day the goddess
rubbed salt and tsabola
in your grievously wounded and bleeding heart.
Your eyes swam in a salt lake of tears
and left a trail of grey grains as they dried.
I, surely, cannot wait to see the good morning
or is it afternoon, evening or night
when the child Chilungamo will be born.

Where Will You Be?

Francis Moto

Where will you be, when the strings
can no longer stand the weight of reason?
We see the rays of the setting sun
slicing the darkness of the forest of deceit.
The passing wind whispers to the leaves
telling the tale of a lion that has lost its mane.
Where will you be when the sharp blade
of your cruelty will have been blunted
by the instruments of justice?
My thoughts dance in circles and settle
on the sharpened edge of the horizon.
They bleed.
The white mist hanging over the hills
still veils my vision of a new tomorrow
When we, the wobbly gazelles,
shall dance the big dance reincarnated
at the sacred shrine of Mankhamba.

I saw the man of darkness today
and his lying face told it all.
If it had been the moons past
I would have sung a song
in the forest of fear.
For a time my hopes dangled low
with the hanging clouds of uncertainty.
But where will he be when the children know
who killed the chidangwaleza
that now roams the village of flames
and threatens to plunge it into endless songs
about the circles we drew
with the chidangweleza's crimson blood?

In my dancing thoughts of a strange dawn
caress the edges of the village
and the morning dew
embraces the children's soft soles

as they, in new found ecstasy, sing of
the ndondocha on the path from the grave.
We knew you would come back one day.

At the moment my mind takes off on a trip
to the ancient hills there to ask
what gave birth to the chidangweleza
and where she will be, when the rays
of the setting sun slice the darkness
of the forest of deceit
and the whispering leaves,
again, tell the tale of a lion
that has lost its mane while it slept?

Where will you be, when the sun has finally set?
Lines simmering with poetry will still be there
to remind you of the ancient wisdom
you so arrogantly spat on.

Sister, we know that your head is an empty basket
for you have failed the test of a passing time.
You look with that killing look but you see not.
You hear with those cocked ears but do not listen.
These lines will still be there when
the spirits have you at their command.
We, the wobbly gazelles, shall still be there
to dance our dance
in the circles of a changed time.

Songs from the Anthill

Francis Moto

In silence the village elders sat under
the shadow of the village by the anthill.
They sat down weaving a tale about
days passed in silence.
And they sat down weaving a tale
about the echoes of voices in the night that
erased smiles from people's faces.
A lament from the anthill rode on the lips
of an orphaned child.

> They buried my father without rites
> after spearing him with a blade of fear.
> They buried my father without beating
> the drum of the big dance.
> My mother's joy they exiled.
> Father and mother, please, help me
> clip the claws of the lioness.

In silence the village elders traded glances
as a widow's lament shot sharp arrows
at the blunted conscience of the lioness:

> You who drank sour palm wine
> to wash down your heavy consciences,
> for my father's honours clipped
> by the claws of the young lioness,
> prepare for the dance of tears
> when your joys will be banished
> into the exile of time.

In silence the village elders saw
smoke rise from the anthill.
And eyes of initiates saw scarlet blood
mixed with grains of water
plus the shadow of a corpse smiling

at the chief of the village elders.
Then from the anthill rang a sorrow-ridden
song of a young man:

I am hunting for an old woman
whose nose dripped of smoke-stained
mucus but cured me of a childhood pain.
I hear she was banished from existence
for asking about her son.

I am hunting for a young woman
whose smile peeled off endless layers of pain
off my heart when you, village elders,
had condemned me to the pits
of eternal darkness.

The village elders scratched their greying
thoughts and listened on:

With me I carry sap
from veined leaves in the hills
shown to me by the old woman
whose nose dripped
of smoke-stained mucus.
With herbs from the forest
of fertile ideas, we are dancing
on a pathway armed to clear
the endless spider's cobwebs.
And with the ashes of the webbed foot
of the chameleon sprinkled
in the drink of ancient poets,
our cracked throats are poised
to sing melodies during the dance
of the rebirth at Kaphirintiwa.

Wrap the heat of your loins
in the soft cloth grandmother
wove under the cool shade
of the village tree.

Time has come for the village
to fold its courage and in it
wrap the shame of a time lost
when we were knotted to a curse
by the spider's web thrust
upon us by fate.

Go
and tell
the children of
the village that the
dry brown pods of silence
exploded scattering seeds
of endless time into the horizon
of fresh hopes. Go and tell the
village maidens that the blood they
forcedly shed was used to wet the sand
with which we baked the bricks to build
a monument of remembrance for a time
when we buried our elders without rites
and a time when nights listened to
the sound of songs wrapped in perpetual
voices of the silent pain of orphaned
children, widowed mothers and cursed
young men with heat in their loins.

Escorting the Mother of Years
Francis Moto

Standing by the banks
of the stomach-turning Thames waters,
I gazed at the setting sun
as seconds chased minutes
and minutes chased hours
for them to chase days
and the days to chase
the final week of the final moon
of the annus horribilis.

Exhausted leaded and unleaded petrol
fought for first positions
in the race to make holes in the ozone.
Christmas gift hunters
disturbed by sirens
rushing to spots of threatened security
shivered the year out as
I stood by the banks
of the nauseating waters of the Thames
watching seconds chasing minutes
and minutes chasing hours
for them to chase days
and the days to be on the heels
of the final week of the final moon
of the mother of all years.

As I watched the excitement
escort the mother of years
into the pages of history
a picture about the hills of home
began to take shape on one
of the billboards.

In that picture I saw a stubborn rebirth
of trees on the hills robed
in velvet purple

after the summer fires
had eaten away their browning leaves.

I saw a man clad in white
rebaptize the hills
by their sacred ancient
names of Chitambe and
Kadamsana

As the billboard advertised
the new female condom
I heard the chanting of prenatal anthems
and advice of where umbilical cords
and the afterbirths should be buried
after the rebirth
of a lost cycle of time.
From the gorges of the hills
I heard songs about
abandoned bags of silence
during an existence of broken dreams.

The village elders beat
their shaven heads
and spoke of high priests
of an imported oracle
who cut the web of silence.

As the waters rolled by
I saw in my mind
the bottled anger
which had flooded the clan's pathways
During the season of the cold winds.
I also saw the dancing on the graves
of the village poets
hurriedly exiled from existence
and velvet monkeys which were accompanying
the mother of all years into the chapters
of what might have been.

At the screeching of hasty taxi tyres
I saw village ghosts as old as the moon
dancing on the roofs of the village elders' huts
while midwives recorded prenatal groans
on the scale of cursed dreams and
sang songs about words that had been strangled
but had now escaped into the ring
of a changing season.

The taxi gone,
the billboard showed the season following
the bonfires the trees on the hill
dressed in robes of velvet purple.

This time the fire
had eaten our rippling shame.
And the changing season
had wiped our bruised silence.
The robes of velvet purple wrapped
our cringing pain in the pods of time
as I escorted the mother of all years
into the horizon of cyclic time.

Children of the Sahel

Lupenga Mphande

Hurtling close, racing to rendezvous
with godfather sun, early risers
watched the comet's display
of divine flickers;

Some said it was an omen
for Sahel children
Who twist and desiccate amidst
carcasses and wilted plants;

Others said it was really
just specks of dust speeding past
from beyond, with a bit of light, perhaps,
reflected from solar planets:

And I say if children of the Sahel are dust,
as they are, and dust rises, as it will,
then they will rise and coalesce,
cuddled in the beyond as comets to stars.

The Lakeside Lady
Lupenga Mphande

I, even I, am he knows the paths
Through the plateau, of whose breeze I breathe

I have beheld the lady of the shimmering lake
I even I, who gallops with the zebra
Emerald blue and foliage green are her clothes
Trailing the adulations as she wades down the escarpment

I even I, am he who knows the paths
Through the plateau, of whose breeze I breathe

I scouted the lady swimming with the fish at dawn
I, even I, who gallop with the zebra
Ivory white are her teeth and jingling bells her voice
Rising above the waves of the lake to re-echo the breeze

I, even I, am he who knows the paths
Through the plateau, of whose breeze I breathe

I saw the lady of the lake hunting with the bee
I, even I, who gallop with the zebra
of mountain dun is her tan and mtowa tree her bow
Her arrows shine silver shaft in the flicker of dawn rays

I, even I, am he who knows the paths
Through the plateau, of whose breeze I breathe

Song of a Prison Guard

Lupenga Mphande

I can see you prisoner of Dzeleka
From behind this hole here in the door panel;
I lurk along the hum of cicadas and mosquitoes
From moonshades of maize stalks and banana leaves
And shadows of barbed wire posts and farm ridges.
I hide behind this iron cleft, this hole, and
Peep into your cell like a Cyclop, unseen
I am guard to this humid valley prison camp.

Your little room prisoner of Dzeleka
Will grow for ever small, your life left in the lurch to waste
And cluck at the wind, even at night I will keep you awake
With this dry doublelock designed to lacerate sweet sleep,
Don't tell me the political layout of your crimes,
I only light the furnace for those I receive to roast
In chilly cells, and I whet the axe for the condemned
To throttle at the gallows like a chick with its head off
I am the guard charged with executions.

Do you see that window up the cell wall
Prisoner of Dzeleka? Of course it's too small and will for ever
Grow smaller, but look out sometimes on some fine days;
If you find it painful to see children at play, and
Watch the life you have so unwittingly deserted, then study:
Count threads in a cobweb, study the beams in a ray from
That crack on the eastern wall at the break of day
And study the ray that lingers on after nightfall,
Study the strands in a life that lost its shadow, study.

When you discover the beam-wave that relates to your pain
Then hum in harmony with cicadas and mosquitoes in the dim
Celebrate the merge of darkness with noon, do a dirge to
The gods of swamps and hillcaves, take three steps forward
Then backward and swerve: weather changes in circles, dawn

Will oust darkness-tropical summers are hot, but your
Cell will for ever be a cold, cold witner. You'll
Live in this narrow room endless hours to the fatal night.
It's like a piece of thread on which our days hang
Stringed to fall away, wasted.

When the Storms Come
Lupenga Mphande

In time
    the sea will wash away the stain
    leaving the gash
    Putrified and impossible of dress

    I am the blank between the colours'
    I am the interspace between the tongues
    I am the one that foresees the end

In time
    the lake will surge
    tossing the pots
    gullying the soil
    in mid-current red showers

I am the blank between the colours
I am the interspace between the tongues
I am the one that foresees the end

In time
    the storm will come
    flooding the shore
    the plateaux and mountains will crumble
    and level in the tribal confragration

I'll be the blank between the colours
    the interspace between the tongues
    the one that will foresee the end.

The Dwarf of the Hillcaves
Lupenga Mphande

There lived a celibate of the hill at home.
One day in a frenzy he dreamed visions
of a race of magicians who could boost
his dwarffish poise and patched domain;

He hastily retired up into his hillcaves
To revel in the cabbala and evoke the mountain gods
To reveal to the world their unique potency from
flywhisks and yoghurt from gyrating maidens;

Sacrifices complete and libation poured to the hill gods
Off he went on a quest to the west, to dip the charmed
root into moulds of the dinosaur and drink rat urine
in accordance with the whispers from the mountain patrons;

When he returned, infested with lice and maggots
and his bag bulging with foreign roots and charms
potent in wild dreams and fantasies the transformation
was complete; people locked to him spellbound

To revel and gyrate all night to the occult
of the hillside caves, while the little man of the hill
snatched and wrung their bodies for yoghurt ingredient
To add to his prescriptions and attain height.

Malawi Poetry Today
Edison Mpina

My name is Edison Mpina. I am phoning you
from a country called Malawi. We
call our country the warm heart of Africa, and
it can be rediscovered faster on the map by following
with a finger the western and northern boundaries of Mocambique,
the eastern boundary of Zambia and the southern boundary of Tanzania.
This is so because Malawi is a small country,
in the shape of a lizard with
a creative population of 7,000,000.
I am a born-poet and I am phoning you to discuss the poetry of my country.
It has no mines
All its industries are primary
It has several mountains
Black soil
Four lakes
Rivers
From which we draw bellyfuls of food.
Our rivers Shire, Linthipe, Songwe and Chimbamera among others
are unnavigable,
but they provide sweet drinkable waters all year round.
Our game parks, Lengwe, Lifupa, Vwaza teem with zebra, cheetah, lions,
leopards and other animal species.
Summer and winter are our only seasons, kind seasons I must say,
they remove their hats when they see us.
Let me say a word more about the seasons, do you hear me?
Okay. Our winters never record large minus statistics.
The leaves on the trees are green as paint, and
we pluck a lot of tea and tobacco for export during winter.
So you can see that we do fly outside the borders of our country
Our summers never record large plus statistics.
Leaves turn brown on the trees, before falling off. Is this not a winter
characteristic in cold countries, I understand?
Summery haze clothes Zomba, Mchinji, Thyolo and other mountains while
the bougainvilleas that swish songfully in winter take a rest.
Like an electric light switched off.
In summer the water on the lakes is theraupetic to swimmers, canoe

rowers and people who come to visit us from other countries.
At night our edible insects which fry as well as sausages, *bwanoni, maathi,*
ngumbi race round our kerosene-lamp-lights and our clean moon,
in search for something more than light. Here's where we catch them.
But is this, you may be asking yourself, poetry? Yes, it is poetry.
All the 7,000,000 inhabitants of my country live in
small villages. In houses made of mud and thatched with grass or palm or
banana fronds,
and the music of smoke curling from our rooftops at sunset,
the smell of five-seven-ten years old, foot-long
threads of smoke dangling as if by magic from our ceiling-less kitchen
roofs, thuds of rats' feet, flaps of cockroaches, ensemble
compose our poetry.
This is what I am discussing.
We live in our fields most of the day.
Hoeing Reaping Weeding Grafting Prunning Tending
Because we believe that to mould good verse, poets must first learn
and master the craft of rearing animals, birds
plants and
In the evenings we dance to *Chopa, Nganda, Malipenga*; and listeners to our
songs from the mouth, from the tom-tom, from the two-string box guitar
solemnly concur that we sing more rhythmically
that any bird symphonies known to them.
We recount and listen to the stories of Mount Malawi in Nsanje,
the hot but fresh springs of Nkhotakota, the craggy
but uniform Rift Valley in Ncheu,
the historic but tragic Lomwe migration from Mocambique,
and the brow-raising story of Mchochoma's discovery of my footprints
and the tracks of many of nature's forms shapes animals
at Kaphirintiwa.
And the great Chewa trek to our country from Congo.
Folds of years ago.
Malawi then, is a country of 7,000,000 poets.
It is easier to become a poet in Malawi than to become anything else,
we observe, because the natural materials for building
poetry are, like wintry clouds, in limitless supply.
Without mines then, we never live thousands of feet underground. Hence
never miss sounds, we never miss sights:
summer fires burning on the slopes of Mulanje mountain

waves forming and breaking and writing names on the sandy shores of Lake
Malawi at Cape Maclear
Floods washing our villages away in the Lower Shire
Flint stones at Nkhoma and other places producing water
And leafless trees of paper at Vinzara letting cold winds pass.
Everything we look at we hear we feel
booms with our poetry.
In my hand I hold a small yellow book simply entitled MAU.
It is a collection of poems by Malawi University students, edited by
themselves and published in the late sixties or thereabouts.
Were our students at that time taught that the craft of verse was the property
of the University,
or were they at least assured of the takeover of poetry by the University,
you ask?
You should ask THEM really, although I am myself aware
of Theodore Weiss's comment that in 'an increasingly unliterate, if
not illiterate, age where else can poetry be preserved?'
Personally I find Weiss's comment that in'an increasingly unliterate, if
not illiterate, age where else can poetry be preserved?'
Personally I find Weiss's point wry.
So, I cannot answer for THEM, much as I have to be brief, this being
a wireless discussion.
MAU means WORDS in the Chewa language of Malawi.
Itself compact, the word MAU is smooth thorny unbroken sensual
It is full of something, like a seed.
MAU then is our near definition of our poetry.
Why near definition?
Because we are still trying to
reach a definition of poetry as it is not easy for a conference of 7 million
poets to reach an agreement, let alone on the perfect definition of
their own poetry in 7,000,000 years.
Is that clear now?
So each one of us 7 million Malawians is chopping one cedar.
To find a vivacious word to describe the silt.
To find a hard word to relate how someone met death.
To find a feathery word to reach at the beauty, the tenderness in skin or
the angelic posture of his new-born son.
To find an ashen word to warn his neighbour about an impending raid
on their cows, dance-words, healing-words death-words.

180

To find a word in the snuff-bins settled for years on the noses of
our senior citizens.
Or the words of crickets bivouacking in the tall grass.
To find these words then, we search our cotton fields in Machinga with our
hoes.
We search our woods at Chikangawa
with our pangas.
we prowl lakes Malawi, Chirwa, Chiuta and Malombe
with our dug-out canoes.
To live a full life of words. Melody life.
The yellow anthology I told you about then is, I think, appropriately
entitled by its student-editors.
From the objects we see and from the sounds we hear:
rusling elephant grass, raging *Mwera*, hissing *Chiperoni* and revving
NAPOLO;
green *mpiru* and air chasing itself over the Nyika Plateau;
from the summer flames of Bwanje Valley (ku Malawi)
we make words we make our poetry we make our life
We do not make our verse from volcanoes erupting in our minds.
Or from isms seen through glass. Imported glass.
Or from THE
But from tangible words.
Our words become our poems. The poems become our words.
Which we own as we own cats. As we own gardens. As we own children.
As we own fetishes
We caress our words as if they were puppies
We swallow them as we swallow berries
We apply words as cosmetics
As hand lotion
Lipstick
We cut words as we cut scarification marks
On our faces On our thighs On our cheeks
Because our very souls lie in our words.
Because in our words lie our very souls.
I am saying that our eyes, ears, noses. Like rotten brain.
The reverse of this process is what I am phoning about.
You are so silent, are you still there? Ok.
All we do in Malawi is season what we hear see smell with our imagination.
Imagination as a poetic component? Exactly. I like that, thanks. That's

the pigment of our words, and one seed of our poetry.
Because it is not a poetry that comes from physiological deeps.
Like a mouse from a hole.
Like a cockroach from a crack in the wall.
Nor like a game of cause-effect between the moon and the mind.
Because it is not a poetry that is given birth in a workshop.
Like a coffin, complete with formica.
Because it is not a poetry that leans on a stick.
Like an old man.
Because it does not have to be suspending all of, and for its life.
Like an avocado pear.
Our poetry is like any acacia, standing on its own roots. Fighting the wind.
It enters into our eyes as arrows.
Into our ears as the buzzing of bees.
It affects our skins as itch-beans.
A sting of a mosquito.
A huge bluegum tree falling on a hut in which an old woman is sleeping.
As a ten pound hammer on a loaf of bread.
Our poetry has nothing to do with Keats, Larkin, Stevens names, Neruda.
Enright, Ginsberg or New York City.
Nothing to do with Auschwitz,
Marcos, Nicaragua or Cape Canaveral.
Nothing to do with King Claudius's speech in Hamlet.
For which reason a professor of poetry in Malawi has neither classroom
nor student to listen to his technical yarns.
Because all Malawians are poet-peasants, poet
students,poet-leaders, poet-followers, poet-teachers and poet-poets.
Oh yes, poet-poets, I said.
This does not mean that we outlawed winged words in our country.
We have winged words in Malawi.
But these are the MAU of those who live in the textile
mills of David Whitehead. In the liquor breweries of
Carlsberg and Chibuku and *Kachasu*.
In the sugar refineries at Sucoma and at Dwangwa.
In the laboratories and operating theatres at Kamuzu Central Hospital
The dressing rooms at Khonjeni Health Centre.
Not in our poetry
Because our poetry refines our systems.

182

Affords passage to our green blood through our green veins.
And opens our eyes to see behind Mulanje mountain, below Mafisi River,
and deep down our souls.
The aim of Malawi Poetry Today is not just poetry,
as Pushkin said, as Delvig believed, and as those in Zomba might
have nodded at the late sixties or thereabouts.
Our poetry throbs.
To make life in Malawi livable.
One more word about the gentlemen of the University.
They pluck the hackles the ailerons the plumage of our poetry
and they paste labels to them with glue. Green labels. Brown labels.
Gold labels. Black labels. Like the brands of Carlsberg.
Our creative beer.
They parse our poetry and give it names: Apollonian. Confessional. Elegiac.
Nonsense. Beat. Mountain.
But all this is mere cataloguing, not versifying.
Because the common Malawians who make our poetry have nothing with
terms used in preserving our poetry in Zomba. Our poetry preserves itself
in the life Malawians lead from day to day.
Its rhythm
Its people
Its geography
Its history-in-making
Its everday
Poetry prostrate on the ground
flapping on the trees
Plastered on the walls
Waving on rooftops
Intoned
Our
Not FOR
The common property of all.
Not the common property of one man in Thyolo.
Lilongwe. Ndirande. In Katawa. In St. Mary's. In Naisi.
Not the property of the person wearing a tweed jacket, or that wearing
suede shoes, or that
wearing
It is the property of 7,000,000 Malawians loving
together, throwing their pestles in tuneful turns, smiling in

waves or weeping in songs.
Hallo, hallo, hallo!
Your want to know my role in Malawi Poetry Today?
Okay.
Because Malawi Poetry is a collective property,
I am only
its representative,
a spokesman for 7 million poets!

Tea Plantations
J.J. Msosa

A sinister green
At dusk and dawn
Evil smelling
Like a healer's concoction
And I wonder
How wiser
The tea shrubs are
After listening
To the silent songs
Of the tea pluckers.

Song of Tinkenawo

J.J. Msosa

For many seasons
Have I followed this lonely path
Climbed the mountains of wisdom
Gone down the valleys
of self torture
Onto the plains of insecurity
of this lonely path
Have I learnt to hate them
Those who bore me
Those who saw me grow
Because they could not
With me climb
Onto the mountains of wisdom
Nor with me come
Down the valleys
Of self torture
Nor with me travel
Through the plains of insecurity
I do remember
That season I left home
The season of sweet smelling
And steaming indigenous dishes
The season of sweet and steaming
Musical nights
But this lonely winding path
Exhausted has left me
Can I appreciate
The very concoctions
That nourished my very soul
A prodigal son I know
I am not

But whenever down I sit
To rest
Or down I lie
To sleep
I hear them call
My kinsmen calling

My clan calling
"Return from the winding path!"

II

Across the ocean
My destination lay I thought
Many seasons gone by
The umbilical cord of my memory
Long and thin was stretched
Over oceans of time and distance
Still I heard them call
Calling after me
But here I am
In thought ragged
In action more ragged still
And when to dine I sit
Or to dance I stand
Or to speak I open my mouth
I hear them call
For the journey
Maimed has left me
In need of crutches of wisdom.

I saw it
Khumbula Munthali

When suggestions were being made
I was there
When the final step was agreed
I was there
When they went to his house,
When they were dragging him out
When they tied his hands, feet,
blind folded him
bundled him into the boot of a car,
I saw it.
When they, without any noise,
moved away
I followed them
When near a river they
Stopped, came out, opened the boot
Benja started to struggle
They needed blows to silence him
Whatever they did to him
So swift, so dramatic.
What did they
do that I fail to account for?
Benja went numb,
they packed him
and tied him in a sack...
I saw it all,
I saw it.

For Ayeyo who was
Ian Musowa

When Ayeyo was Chief
wild beasts scattered dust in flight
and people with beasts' hearts/helter-sketter disappeared
thus he relieved his people of
their sorrows and burdens.
(You see they used to labour
making gigantic contour ridges
in virgin bushes for a few
whips and scolds.
Your see they used to snarl
at each other,
could even gouge out
each other's eyes!
You see they used to display
their genitals
not to excite each other
but POVERTY ruled this).
All that died
and all was silence
tense silence
guarded by I-will-report-you-eyes
and wagging of fingers
as warning and threats
which often ripened!
He said
he and his people
were like death and man
never would they part
till death did them.

And now death did them part
and the people red-eyed;
with years of mourning
are still red-eyed with
ABHORRENCE

for Ayeyo.
Didn't sweat like King Henry Eight
to reap an heir they say,
and some wonder if he
didn't plan it that way
the castrated bastard so that
We must say this BLACK would
have been WHITE if Ayeyo were here.
Too much Energy in us Destroys

Too much energy destroys us and others
To F. Mzoma
Sam Raiti Mtamba

and too little of it
drives lambs from their homes
running away from leonine neighbours
To come back certainly
lambs turned into lions
storming their canine neighbours for survival.

II

You see my ancestors once feared and revered mountains:
The pithy heart of the mass of rock, trees, streams
Had more than ordinary power, they said. And every once in a long while
Napolo, that huge water snake from the caves of the mountain
Fuelled by the punitive spirits of our forefathers
Stormed down a century of wrongdoing
relentlessly in the plains below. These days of course
Mountains are mere mountains
Sins committed reach no further
than the tallest house
We've tucked justice under our very own armpits.
The energy is ours, the power ours
We can do anything
Without fearing a landslide, exploding rocks
Or lakes of water, sweeping the jacaranda and acacia incensed
City in the planes
Down to the sea

To a Black American Brother
Geoff Mwanja

What makes you turn your back on me saying
with blind emphasis:-
"My grandmother was a Red Indian
I've no black blood in my veins."

For you are as black
as your comb-refusing hair,
Clumped in curls
like trees on Ndirande hill.
Your nose is big and flat
Your lips, thick and curly
Your eyes, dark and gleaming.

What makes you say this?
Is it the Nsima you just ate
tasteless to you
and the concrete pavements you miss?
Or is it the small boys you see playing
with a rag, their limbs dusty?

****

Emigrant Pole

Anthony Nazombe

I can see your figure silhouetted
Against the skyline as you trudge
Across the mountain range
Into exile, weighed down by children
And suitcase bursting with bread and underwear.
Only the music concealed in the blade of the wind
Soothes your brittle ears; fleeting airs
Of the Messiah salve your chapped lips
And massage your fluttering heart.

I can see you standing in the lengthening queue
Outside that embassy, your feet sore and eyes red
For lack of sleep; you shuffle forward,
Every step bringing you nearer the gift
Of another life. Oh! How thankful you must be
That earth still breeds men of goodwill;
Your lungs swell with the tones of the Magnificat
And your face with blessedness.

But, sweet woman, I fear for you,
I dread the road your feet have chosen;
For there is no rest where it leads.
I have seen the shepherd in Rome
Lash the marauding soldiers in your land
Till they squirmed and cried, 'Enough!'
Yet not once has he stopped to look which way
His panicking flock is fleeing,
And in desperation some of the sheep have grown
Strong claws and an insatiable appetite for flesh;
See how they migrate south, stalking African herds!

I fear for you, apprentice huntress,
For already the veld is ablaze,
The spirits of the land have awoken

From countless seasons of slumber
And even now the predators are in full flight,
scampering towards the sea,
Where they will certainly perish
Unless the bald eagle comes to their rescue.

Modes of Freedom
(After Annemarie Heywood)
Anthony Nazombe

My mind floats clear of steel bars
Blocking the vision of the inmate,
Flapping wings sedately and leisurely
Against the vast blue dome
Now tinged with the crimson twilight.

Above the bluegum trees
Crows hover, matching feather with feather
Before disappearing into their nests;
Down below late shoppers gingerly weave their way
Through terraced birdshit.

Nobody really bothers about these scavengers
Only the occasional curse when the paste
Scores a direct hit or even laughter
At being caught off one's guard.

Crouched as if in readiness for evensong,
A man scribbles his pain on the walls
In the ramshackle toilet behind the banana stall:
a combination of big-bellied b's and backward-looking s's.
Momentarily relieved, he returns to his post
At the entrance to the banquet hall of the father.

As the mellow morning light seeps through
Layers of foliage, monkeys scale the walls
Round State House to play hide-and-seek
At the meeting-point between branch and barbed wire;
Ignoring the nervous barks of neighbourhood dogs,
The scouts calmly peer into the recesses of power.

But the guards look elsewhere,
Scanning the mountain road
For daring photographers or bottoms
Swinging under the weight of firewood

I am trotting past the main gate
When a cunning sociologist inquires:
"Where are you coming from, Chief?"
Inspired by mischief, I reply:
"I went up to collect new tablets of law."
You should see him dashing off.

Blind Terror

Anthony Nazombe

Death came hidden under the hand
Of this blind man
He strayed into our house one night
Looking for guidance;
But, hand searching beyond the staff,
He strangled this sister of mine.
She wailed to the sky and to the earth
As her brothers looked on paralysed.

After the scream to deafen death
Came the weight of silence
And that face of stone
Disappeared in the gloom
Leaving wailing in its wake.

He came again through the door
Groping about and rattling his staff
Again seeking a guide;
Before mother could shout or move
His left hand silenced this brother of mine
Again there was a corpse on our hands.

Mother wept, we all wept
Hurling impotent curses
At the blind salesman of death.
Mother implored,
Clinging to the last born,
"Child, that you may not die!"

But in a mirror I saw death
Spring from the hand of this blind man
Weaving through the living
To fall on those he had already marked;
In vain had mother hidden them.

I feared death
From the groping hand
And the rattling staff;
I feared the unseeing eyes
And the unfeeling face.

I shuddered to think I might be blind
Sowing death among the seeing
All the time only seeking a guide.

This Temple
Anthony Nazombe

This temple you are about to enter
Through outstretched tongue
And half-closed eyes,
This temple is unclean.
Layers of dust dating back
Half a decade lift and dance
In rays that filter through
Cracks in the boards.
I am not worthy to receive you;
My lips tremble, my nose twitches
As the lore of wizards dropping dead
At the raising of the host
Or laymen stricken dumb by the power of the grail
And palms the wafer bored through,
Blood and water collecting where it melted,
Haunts me from the days of my youth.

A pilgrim from the north, I have presumed
For the sake of this child whose tones of the wilderness
Echo as salt touches his lips
And spring water soothes his brow.
Let me lace his shoes and gird his loins
When he begins to cleanse our pig-sties
In readiness for your second coming.

Song for a Hunter
(for Lupenga)
Anthony Nazombe

Your days are gone, master stalker of Bunda;
The lions and elephants that ravage this land
Are far too subtle for your bow and arrows
And even if they weren't, your rival,
That upstart from the hill-caves
Who wandered the whole world
In the quest for an elder's head,
Would quake at your echoing crow.
I see you bent-backed in exile

Who gave your name to rolling plains
Cleaving the kingdoms of Mbelwa and Mpezeni
Hunter for all seasons keeping at bay
The mighty regiments of Zwangendaba.
Now you wait for the sinking sun

At the foot of Mulanje Mountain
In a travesty of a zoo
Built in the years of *thangata*
To facilitate the collection of tax
What twist of fate brings you here
Who once accepted the stool of chiefship
From a people overwhelmed by gratitude?

Your days are gone, master stalker of Bunda,
Whose stunning speed on the battlefield
Was matched by the patience of a tortoise,
Unravelling the tangled tongues of men
Undere the shade of the Kachere tree:
The aggrieved went home laden with goats
The wicked repaired to their huts wiser men.

Tuberculosis

Anthony Nazombe

It begins all the way down the lungs
Like a whirlwind or a storm
Seething upwards, gathering momentum
Exploding in the throat like thunder
The spittle, sapping blood and weight,
Flows into spittoon-under a lid
And I await another quake.

Yes, it has always been like this
Inhaled and exhaled
Only at first words flowed instead
And, finding no lid, rode on the wind
To invade other chests.

Same say fresh air is all we need,
Two or three months on a mountain top
But such air is hard to get
And we live quarantined in this ward
Bored with counting our ribs
Awaiting another quake.

News from outside, brought
By new members of this club,
Points to multiple accusations
Of the kind "Who has jumped who?"
But even suspects carry the symptoms.
Then they blame the eastern wind;
Coughs burst on their lips
And the spray claims more victims.

Sometimes when the whooping stops
We read texts from the Bible,
Sent to us by pastors we have never seen,
To fight against the malady.
Plans are underway for a church of our own,
With a shepherd from this flock,

So we can go, after the last quake,
To spread the Word among those outside.
We hope they won't persecute us,
Fearing the Word is infected.

Misty Presences
Anthony Nazombe

I have heard them trudging along the gravel path
In the small hours of the morning
Misty presences murmuring in the wind
Across streams, through labyrinths
Of matchbox huts and waking markets
Travellers from the rim of the city
Earmarked long ago for swift demolition
Yet proliferationg to panic proportions
Till a hedge vainly seeks to obscure the view
From incoming tourists and guests;
They have trodden through my dreams
Marching as to war in discarded boots
To feed conveyor belts at the heart of the web.

Battle for Chingwe's Hole

Anthony Nazombe

I

Laughter issues from the cavern below,
The wicked peals of Namarohi
Lying on an ancient bed of navel strings.
He who came into the world
Complete with teeth, a grey beard and a tail,
Who strutted in the midst of controversy
As old wisdom recommended his death,
Claiming he was a sign of the times
When dead trees arose to take their former places
And locusts stood poised on the horizon.
Laughter spills out of the hollow below,
The convulsive guffaws if a dwarf possessed:
"Who told you that witches plummetted this way once
Or that my path leads too Scylla and Charybdis?
Which grandmother poking at burnt potatoes
Ever sang of the Christian God
Meeting his death on these heights
To redeem the victims of Arab slavers?
Brood of deserters, must you purge
Your guilt over my shaven head,
Blame your misfortunes on speechless depths?
Whatever happened to the nantongwe ritual
That, shameless tourists all,
You should flock here for a cure?
Has the nankungwi abdicated
In preference for a Party post?
Then go seek him at this year's state banquet,
Tell him I am the one reminding him of his burden;
For I shall not have invalids for warriors
When the season of bloodshed comes round again."

II

Who in the year of famine
Summoned the best drummers

And after a month of dancing
In the village square
Led his people to the banks of the Mnembo.
How we gyrated that time
Oblivious of pangs of hunger,
Limbs lifting despite themselves,
Compelled by the magic tail of Namarohi.
We danced till the moon hung over the waters,
Watched as the bearded dwarf, our chief,
Hacked a path through the torrents.
First the drummers, followed by the women,
Babies strapped onto their backs,
Heads laden with baskets and pots;
Then the men, axes on their shoulders,
Spears or pangas in their hands
(Some carried guns from Mbwani);
Namarohi brought up the rear
And the water closed over his head.
For many days and nights
We danced on the banks of the Mnembo
To the rhythm of submarine drums
That grew fainter with each sunset;
In their wake our fishermen
Reported baskets of smoked *chambo*
Found floating on the waters.

III

Who tore the hair from his chest
When Mapantha, that interpreter from Tchinde,
Beguiled Khumbanyiwa into surrendering the land
To the Portuguese intruders and their sepoys
In exchange for coats and calico.
The duped ones clapped their hands and chanted:
Pwiya, pwiya,nnokhwelani nyuwano!
But whose grand-father's spirits
Were these monsters from the sea?
Observing this treachery from the mists
Beyond Murumbu Hill, Namarohi sensed

206

In his blood that such folly
Would sap our warriors' morale
In the numerous engagements to come;
He knew too that this was the beginning
of the confusion that still dogs us:
Kuruwe, the place named after its partridges,
Turned into the meaningless Guruwe;
Then our people twisted their captors' tongue
Into words strange enough to send the frogs
On the banks of the Nikhuku
To premature death by drowning:
'Rekoni', 'Karitela', and bloated carcasses
Floated on the once clear waters.
My ancestor descended from the hills
And for a whole year wreaked havoc among the bandits.
Smouldering boma posts marked the route he followed
Behind dispossessed men, women and children
On the westward march to a new home at Nsoni.
But Mapantha, that ubiquitous son of a chameleon,
Was there again to meet them.

IV

Who lured raiding impis into quagmires
Where overjoyed crocodiles found them;
Who in the recesses of Malabvi Hill
Taught a fugitive people
Not only the art of rolling rocks,
But also warfare with couldrons of kalongonda:
The Ngoni regiments of nachikopa fame
Wilted in the very hour of seeming triumph.
When overseas predators fell upon our men,
Pressing them to toil for rolls of tobacco
Or breaking their backs with guns for an alien war,
Namarohi grew restless in the adopted abode;
His memory drifted back in time
To youths dragged from their villages
To sweat it out on the prazos along the Zambezi,
Leaving fields untilled and granaries gaping.

Where on earth could a man find peace?
He was there at the secret meetings
As the elders cracked the riddles of the new age;
When the kernel pointed to the sharpening of spears,
He it was that supervised the taking of the oath
And the departure of couriers,
All this against the carnival background of tchopa.
With ground herbs from Murumbu he put to sleep
Plantation owners, DC's and the Governor,
Who saw and smelt the smoke of battle
Yet continued to frequent waterholes.
The warriors proceeded under cover of darkness
To sever the heads of their tormentors
But those who ventured farthest
Encountered the grostesque grin of a familiar mask:
Mapantha had vanished when he was needed most.
The fleet-footed fled, leaving the dead behind,
Or captives to be shot in the market-place at dawn.

V

Who advised Kaduya on the manner of attack
The day the askaris were routed at Malindi;
But after the tactician had been shot in the leg
And a deserter had alerted the enemy,
My ancestor, master of the underworld,
Guided Chilembwe through thick lines
Of armed zombies and would-be traitors
To a remote island on Lake Chilwa.
Thwarted, the hound-dogs killed a passer-by,
Serving him up to their masters
As the leader of the rebellion:
The white sea-god required a blood sacrifice.
But those who knew the truth
Discreetly visited the lake
Bringing gifts of fowls and flour.
Because his wife had brought death to so many,
He swiftly dispatched her to the spirit world;
As for Mapantha, his harsh ending absolved him:

208

He who had dodged action found it in himself
To make a brilliant defence of the rising
At the moment of reckoning, stunning the inquisitors.
Chilembwe himself died an old man in 1953;
He will come again at the next millennium
When the fat and powerful among us,
Adopting the perverse wisdom of Livingstone,
Once again appropriate the land
That so many bled and died for,
Urging the rightful owners to work it for them
In the name of progress.

VI

Namarohi then fought on the side
Of the young men of the forest,
Sojourned under stagnamt pools,
Breathing through reed snorkels,
Till mouldy boots bred worms
And the skin peeled off the warriors' feet.
Those were the years when,
Possessed of the madness of dogs,
The sepoys used pregnant women for target practice
And set fire to wailing children.
Lately he fought in the battles
Of the century old Chimurenga,
Dug tunnels into prison villages
And redistrubuted the recaptured land;
His tail still smarts
Where stray shrapnel pierced it.
In memory of those who fell
He has carved the following:
A woman, child strapped to her back,
Balancing on her head
A delicate bundle of grenades,
And a wounded white soldier
Riding on the shoulders of a native son:
No foreign hosts can ever hope
To triumph over the spirits of the ancestors.

VII

Laughter flows from the depths of the hole
As Namarohi inspects poets
Entangled in the dark legend of Napolo:
Is this perhaps the monster
That unnerved Shaka,
Fold upon endless fold
Protruding above the waters of the Mfolozi
To conjure up visions of empire?
Is this the answer to the riddle
That bounces back from the walls of Chingwe's Hole?
But my ancestor scorns pointless fascination with myth,
Preferring the daring of the latecomer;
Who, in the year of the Great Flood,
Ferried distressed maidens singlehanded
From Mzimu Ndirinde to the shore.
He then followed the subterranean spoor
Of the much vaunted serpent
To its lair in the womb of the mountain,
Challenging Napolo to a wrestling match;
But Alas! The monster was blind,
Massive eyelids closing over empty sockets.
In his hour of shame, Napolo offered Namarohi
Unsurpassable knowledge of herbs.
But my ancestor declined,
Knowing full well the duplicity
Of shattered behemoths.
Yet compassion fell so heavily on the warrior
That he quickly fashioned a bangwe
To play lullabies to the stricken anarchist.

VIII

It is true mountain rivers break their banks,
Brick walls crumble under the onslaught
And the embarrassed residents
Scurry for shelter on hilltops elsewhere.

That happens when Napolo's anguish is too much
For him (such is the weight of enforced idleness)
And he bangs his colossal head
Against the mighty pillars of his den.
That is when Namarohi has put his harp aside,
Temporarily broken off his eerie laughter
And quietly slipped down South
Through subterranean pathways
To check whether the mines he planted years ago
Are now ripe for the final conflagration.
My ancestor chronically chafes at his laurels,
Itching to move on to new battlefields.

Black Cat

Anthony Nazombe

I

I watched, transfixed, as a black cat
Stalked a giant white mouse;
It was carefully edging forward,
Hugging the ground as felines are wont to do.
The prospective victim appeared hypnotized
And curiosity mingled with the predatory urge
In the hunter's eyes.
Suddenly the mouse changed into a mongoose;
The cat drew back in fear
But soon continued circling its protean quarry,
Taking care to skip out of reach
Each time a giant paw lashed out in its direction.
My heart jumped then yet I could not move,
however much I tried,
To steer the cat out of danger.

II

As I watched, transfixed,
A yellow and brown cobra slithered onto the scene;
It made as if to by-pass the stalemated pair
But the mongoose quickly spotted in
And, ignoring the cat, gave chase.
A furious battle ensued as cobra, head raised
Sought to puncture mongoose's coat
Or stamp the light out of his eyes.
But the rodent't mass belied its speed
For it wove magic skeins round the ophidian
And when the trance was complete,
Pounced upon the puffed gullet.
Execution was swift and, as I watched,
The mongoose set about swallowing the cobra
After the manner of a python.
Its limbs expanded with each disappearing coil

212

Until the head had grown threefold
The legs four and the maw five.
The colour of its coat gradually changed;
Yellow and brown spots replaced the white.

III

After its heavy meal the mongoose went to sleep
On its hunches; it had hardly started snoring
When the cat leapt from nowhere
And, as I watched transfixed, opened its mouth wide
And started swallowing the mongoose,
Beginning with the mammoth head.
Before long the cat's head had grown fifteenfold
The legs twenty and the maw twenty-five
The colour of its coat gradually changed
First from black to white
Then to the cobra's yellow and brown.
After its massive meal the giant cat
Issued a blood-curdling battle-cry
Then leapt into the nearest thicket,
Leaving my heart pounding in my ears.

On Reconciliation
(The Hawk, From the Chickens)
Alfred Tyson Nkhoma

You have been commissioners of death
More than three decades stopping our breath
But now let us all flock together

As birds of the very same feather
The manner of this diabolical fight
Would simply make the matter light
Once you cease to undermine us
With you special cheating designs

If you want the everlasting peace
We enjoy in this Kingdom to increase
then refrain from that unexampled greed
and do not aim at profiting always

Then we will live in total happiness
If you will truly stop your madness.

Ring Freedom Bells

Immanuel Bofomo Nyirenda

Trees bow and shake,
dogs bark and stampede,
While ants sing in chorus:
Ring, ring freedom bells.
Let blood flow but Freedom come.

Windows get smashed, barns get looted;
Gangs hold guns
To shoot at the shouting masses
Or blind them with tear gas.
Ring, ring freedom bells.
Let blood flow but Freedom come.

Mountains dance
To the tunes of the mixed choir.
Scared lions run for their lives,
While their females make love to elephants.
Ring, ring freedom bells.
Let blood flow but Freedom come.

Tethered hares and the deer
Join the weaver birds
In making melodies to mankind,
Reminding him of his oppressed status,
For peace and right are stolen from him.
Ring, ring freedom bells.
Let blood flow but Freedom come.

Wearied with Persuasion and flattered with bribes,
Justice gives way
To let Right go in chains into gaol
To toil for the tyrants and please Oppression,
Though innocent and benisoned.
Ring, ring freedom bells.
Let blood flow but Freedom come.
Immanuel Bofomo Nyirenda

Father and son
(Mikuyu detention centre, January 1992)
Patrick O'Malley

I pulled the car into the shade of baobab
And tried to read. This time was different:

My friends had left. One wanders worldwide;
Others wait, wondering what the future holds.

This trip a throw-back. Unable to let go
And relishing familiar routine: recalling
What to bring, how much, and whether
This or that would be allowed.

This time was different!

The boy on an adventure, out of school
Wondering at everything. For how long
Had he known "Your Dad's in prison"?
And what did he expect? "What will
He say to me? Or I to him?"
His elder brother calmed him.

I tried to read. Time passed.
A prisoner helped to carry our largesse.
I watched them turn the corner out of sight
And waited. The children round my car
Marvelled at flashing indicators-
Mechanical distractions passing time.

They came at last, with empty
Bags and baskets. The boy would only
Nod. His brother told the story:

"Our father says to thank you.
It was his first time to see the boy.
He took him on his knees and stroked his hair.
He talked and talked to him and always smiled.
He says that God will bless you."

Desolation
(for Idrissa)
Patrick O'Malley

I watched you turn the soil at the first rains,
I watched you plant the seed, drill after drill
Together we observed the seedlings sprout.

This was a year of promise. The clouds gave birth
And in their wake the maize stalks blossomed.
The hope we shared was everywhere, and we rejoiced
That for this year at least, no ritual lies need sprout.

We welcomed early tassles and began to count:
Last year, five bags; this year? Ten! or Twelve!
Abundance now to nurture all the generations-
Food to spare- you'd told me once, "We never sell!"

All that was weeks ago. Today I passed your garden
And I winced at desolation. The wind made music
In the drills. The green maize you had promised
Mocked me now- aborted cobs swaying in sterile haze.

This morning's paper on the seat blasphemed
In banner headlines "Another bumper harvest!"
A north-bound convoy dazzled me with angry glare
As vultures glided overhead awaiting what
Death throes I dare not contemplate.

Discovery
(Nkhudzi Bay, February 1992)
Patrick O'Malley

Here, too, the waters ebb and flow.

My footprints, sculpted carefully just now
At water's edge have disappeared,
Eroded while I slept.

And I have watched as mini wave on wave
Has clawed its pattern in sands
Old as the hills above.

Canoes, sculpted from single trunk
In time beyond our time glided past.
A waterbird bent on its patient search
Flits in and out, resentful of my presence.
Disturber of the peace, I persevere
Until with angry cry the bird
Takes leave of me.

The flowing tide creeps over bank of sand
And spreads in rivulets wave after mini wave
The climbinng sun drives me into the shade
I pause, remembering how patient observation
Over centuries unravelled mysteries.

Now quantum leaps compound our ignorance.

For Us Who Remain
(Chancellor College, Friday, September, 25th, 1987)
Patrick O'Malley

So what, my friends!
If you and I have some
Unfinished business, it can wait
Today we'll grieve
And rail at all the isms
To which we are in thrall.

We were the music makers
(Once upon a time)
But we went out of tune
Such a long time ago
They have forgotten
We thresh about
In futile disarray
Quixotes on our treadmill
To Emmaus

Today, my friends, let's conjure up
Some far fetched gestures
Let's slaughter skinny animals
In our back yards
Let's peddle groceries
From door to door
Let's mint our souls
For calico
Or - in expansive mood-
Let's shit upon the road
Like Angela.

Or let's pretend

We are the music makers
Let us sing dirges now
For all that was
And for our courage

Let us celebrate
A meaningful parenthesis.

Of course, my friends,
There will be other days.

Three Songs for Jack Mapanje
Niyi Osundare

1

We shall sing this song before the Philistines descend
with creaking cannon and chariots of dusty accent;
we shall sing this song now that handsome sun
unfrowns the sky, vigorous like a seething forge

Their trail is as
their horizon a tattered hem
of trembling skies

> Their soles are deaf
> to the summon of the dew;
> clay dies in their mangling hands

They shoot fat guns at the spine
of tender tomes, garnering trophies
from the pyre of martyred letters

> Theirs is the fire which burns
> without the dancing flame,
> blast of a brute a blinding furnace

We shall sing this song before pounding hooves
drown the drum of seminal seasons;
we shall give a tongue to every wood,
sermon to every stone, shape to every shadow

We shall sing this song before the Philistines descend

2

Octogenarian nights strut the avenues
of our noon,
with manacles in their mein,
screaming skulls their iron gaits

Doddering dreams stalk their visions;
a senile infamy still so strong
in the chronicle of our plastic silence;
eunuch sirens father servile twilights
in the marketplace of striving tongues
will our proverb come back home
without the magic of the uttering mouth?

The messiah once descended,
sweeping through the streets
on the saddle of our cheering shoulders.

The messiah once descended,
in the league of patriots and archpatriots:
the prayers shouted so feverishly
in the tabernacle of departing masters
have found an amen now
behind a bramble of bristling bars
The messiah once descended

Those who shuttered the window against nibbling rodents
have heaved open our door for a cabal of starving leopards

3

Why do you talk in knives now,
Your hands teeming with eggshells
And hot blood from your own chicken?

And the chameleons swallow their gods
And their stomachs turn crimson temples
Of thundering tantrums;
And the gods turn into baobabs
With gargantuan roots,
Then into rocks
Then into elephants
Then into sharks

Which pound the deep like blind mortars

Their chameleons have swallowed a god;
Which dunghill will suffer their squatting pangs?

    *   *   *

We read it in the sky, Jack,
we read it in a board blue with black ciphers;
we read those heiroglyphs scribbled on
the wailing wall of our sombre seasons
we read it from the alphabet of the gun
those crypt-p-grams so sticky
with clots of rifled knuckles

For ours, still, is a season of sirens,
of rainless thunders which massacre
the ears of the moon;
the legs which bathed the innocent camwood
of our cheering dawn
have vanished so soon into castles
of a thousand moats;the legs have vanished
only the boots remain

But beyond these shackled moments,
beyond these stony glares of a tortured sun
the Zomba hills spell the hues of a gathering rainbow

For the chameleon which swallows a god
will find a colourless twilight
at the bottom of Chingwe's Hole

a hole on Zomba plateau into which wrong-doers were dropped. (source:
courtesy Mapanje)

224

For Jack Mapanje (following his release)
Niyi Osundare

And the hawk swooped down
On our precious chick:
It was the hour
Before the sun's frantic dance
To the centre of the sky

Grey-taloned,
The hawk reached for the rib
Of our dream.
But there was no silence
In our house of feathers

Several seasons now
We have measured the moments
Like a mother counting the teeth
Of an only baby.
Time never stood like a bull
Tethered to a tree beyond the sea.
The sky chewed the moons
Forests turned green, then yellow.
We scribbled tender legends
On the foli-age of budding stars
We threw hard songs
Through the window of the sky

Several seasons now
The hawk's cannibal swoop
But there was no silence
In our house of feathers

Those walls
Those barbed edicts
Those tiny cages
Custom-made for the elephant

Of the soul
Those golgothas
Where captured dreams
Fly with broken wings

But somehow HOPE survives
And when the hawk swooped down
On the paradise of our fold
It met no silence
In our house of feathers

We seek no immortality
In grey castles
Or the stained windows
Of bastard basilicas;
We beg no permanence
From the dumbness
Of fabricated idols.
Only this:
that the Word never dies
in our mouths
Only this:
that, with its tempered nib,
we dig every day the tyrant's grave
We whose bread is stone
Must sprout new teeth
For the fest of these unusual seasons

Welcome back, mother's child,
Welcome to this running carnival
Of our wounded laughter.
We will be there
When Time's chameleons
Gobble up the season's gods
We will paint in polyglot colours
The bony parables of Chingwe's Hole.

For when the hawk swooped down
With its grey talons

There was no silence
In our house of feathers.

(May 21, 1991)

The Poem
Aber, Wales, April 89 U.K.
D.B.V. Phiri

A poem, a large poem in me;
I caught it
Or it caught me pretty early I reckon
A large one and hard to tell,
Tell it all

A poem of all that passes under
Flying clouds, still clear sky and
Bright moonlit night;
Of my search with God within
And without; who gets it all right and
Just all right?

Every chapter and every nook
of this subdued yet terribly
Unsubdued work, the cries
Of many who come without a choice or with
the choice of others and yet
left with no choice for the way
In or out

The poem is a passion
It must be or else …
But where are the words with
Which to write it? Where are
The hearts on which to pour it?

Up Constitution Hill
After Aber Constitution hill top, UK.
19/5/89
D.B.V. Phiri

Up high
Where the brain winds
And feet tremble
Where you see the symmetry
Of nature's handwork

Up high Oh! up high where the puzzle of
Bumps and galleys fade
Rubbish and drain unite in beauty
A screen of grey and green

Up high! oh! up high!
The harmony of it all
Inspires a thousand dreams
Life's puzzle
Should be seen like that
Bumps and galleys
Rubbish and drain
Working all for the good.

United in Death

D.B.V. Phiri

The greatest strength is
What lies at the center of it all
At the center of it all is
Common vulnerability and the
Unity in death

I have seen this many times
Several times probably before
But every emotion awaits an outlet

The whales trapped in ice once
broke barriers to unity -
Common vulnerability of
East and West, (North and South)

No Tears of Sorrow
Kadwa Phungwako

Lo! Children of Maravi,
Do not weep, thus saith *Mumbi*;
Your tears of sorrow are not for you,
For across the valley thou shalt rest
Thy grief shalt be no more.

Thy perpetual weariness
Shalt be compensated for;
Thou shalt be rejuvenated
for saith thy God, *Mphambe*.

The viper has lost its fangs
Its sting is no more venomous
Our children shall play in the *Malunja*;
And you shall not need all those bows and arrows
To drive it away.

Behold saith *Namalenga*,
Your sorrows, do not carry across the valley,
For there shall be no darkness,
Thobwa and *Chioda* to the ululation
For the coming of dawn; the vipers there
Will slither harmlessly amidst our children
This had come to pass-thus saith *Chiuta*.

Then The Monster Rose and Failed
Ambokile Salimu

Who said
    Man is a dog
    To be licked up.
    Swallowing empty dogmas
    While bathing in his own
    Urine and blood?

Who said
    The carnivore must starve
    While the hyena belches
    With satisfaction,
    Who?
Encouraging scavengers
To under the tree regurgitate.
This monster: itself the weakness
That eventually hits it - BANG
Then what of the curtain of Iron!

Will all spiders, ants and bees
Build large if not
Equal webs, hills and hives?

Our bearded dreamer -
Four billion limousines and
Four billion mansions
Will never be.
Our short-bearded dreamer,
As you not
    Admit:
It was naivety if not insanity
That excreted the big book.

The book that has
Preserved the camps
And spawned death-
Kampuchea to Managua;

Children soldiers clutching
Kalashknovs as
Students litter Beijing
With their bones,

Justifying the lie,
The mistake of the monster.
But where's that floodlit walk?
Our bearded dreamer;
The audacious big cheeked
One from the East
And of course - the revolutionary mind
From north-East.
We witness another popular revolution:
The wall already fallen,
And oh! the Aryan come-together.
Soon the monster'll
Rot with you.

****

Nation Building (or Crack Filling)

Francis Sefe

Another one has popped
Out of the rot like a worm
Out of a rotten carcass ...

Time for another round
Of ritual stone casting
Public display of skeletons
And ineffectual crack filling.

When will a master builder emerge
To strip this colossal edifice
Threatened by a maze of cracks
To the very foundation ...?

This colossal edifice
Could yet become a mansion
But if an elephant is in a coma
What will it take to revive it?

Demo Crazy
Francis Sefe

It must be madness
When men long forgotten
Come rushing to villages
Whose names now twist their tongues

Looking for their umbilicals
Under every hearth
Extorting titles
Or creating new ones

Squeezing frail hands
That otherwise they
Would not allow
To carry their chamber pots.

And human blood is spilled
As if to authenticate
This masquerade dance
Of returned spirits.

Yet all this is not necessary
The numbers having been pre-decided
Behind closed doors
At the dead of night

Except to satisfy foreign suckers
Who judge a wine by its froth
So they can write tomes
About their democracy in our land.

A View of Lake Malawi
Francis Sefe

Out of Salima
I fell upon a vast expanse
Of formless flats stretching
into communion with the sky.

Suddenly, I found myself dwarfed
by piles of sand arranged in pairs
like breasts on a virgin chest
the road following the mid-groove.

My mind had barely taken in
these wondrous handiwork of Nature
When a cool wind massaged my face
and I turned to behold something even more spectacular.

There, in front of me, lay
infinite blue expanse of water
surveilled by towering guards
breathing water exhaling envigorationg breath.

So gentle, so serene You do not
even announce Your presence like
the brash sea does; neither do You
tumble in rough play like the plebian sea.

You spill over Your rim in gentle spills
tongues of water nimbly twanging
tunes through golden sands -
balmy tunes for wounds innerwards ...

Even the mighty Sun presents
Himself to you each morning
before departing on His daily
travel from horizon to horizon.

I notice you also occasionally take back
What you have given; but that does not
diminish Your beauty; if You did not do that
I would have sworn You were not real.

Unlike the genocide wreaked on Keta
by the sea, You only take back bits as
a gentle reminder to the ungrateful of
Your benevolent Queenness.

Promise me one thing, my Queen:
that You will not cast a furtive glance
at these greedy suitors treading your frontage
until I return with the dowry fit for Queen ...

Disturbing Images ...
Francis Sefe

In these days of multi-speak
and multi-vision
I have taken to seeking the fountain
of words I read and images I see.

Right now I see three saplings on the
front cover of ODI
three saplings growing vigorously
from the depths of fertile earth
suddenly one of them doubles over
and continues growing but earthwards
and I wonder why ...
Has it like a seasoned soldier
surveyed the field and decided
time was not ripe to advance
and so is returning to its trench
to await more propitious times?

Is it going back in protest
or is it indeed dying
after having been shipped a thousand times
sanitized at full strength
by the guardians of thought?

Perhaps it is simply a coward
one of those who don't venture out
because the clouds look ominous
forgetting that it rains even
When the sun is perched high ...

Someone call me Mapanje
Nazombe
Lipenga

Call the Whole lot for me
I have a song which has
travelled the ages
it is for them

At Aklinonu
tears will flow
let cowards return
to their mother's womb
you will sleep in calico
the brave will sleep in desolate lands
wind precedes rainstorm
when rain plays kind and forgets sun
it does so at its own peril
no storm blows kapok beyond the clouds ...

The Shire at Kamuzu Barrage
Francis Sefe

I can't help laughing at your plight,
mighty Shire;
Remember how you used to empty our pot
into the ocean
knocking down our dwellings along the way
sweeping along crops & pets?
Now we've got you; oh, how are the mighty
fallen:
See how tiny metal discs so restrain you
you have to fume & foam
in order to relieve bladder pressures; I can't
help laughing at your plight.
From now on, know that you are the slave and
we the masters:
We shall determine how much piss you send
down your conduit;
We shall control how fast you can run
down your track;
and remember, more importantly, if it pleases us,
we can shut you out of this world completely.

Oh, mighty Shire how can I sympathise with you?
You are like Rain who played King for too long
forgetting Sunshine will return!

The Expatriate
Truth As I See It.
(Version II)
Edwin Segal

My dear students: I see the truth,
but with eyes split between two worlds:
mine and yours, theory and fact.
Market forces grow more maize for
sale, so famine stalks the land,
dry currency crumbles,
and the bankers' dust bowl fills.
What's that you say?
Oh my dears,
I have no answers, only the right
vision. Modern needs destroy tradition.
Families disintegrate into isolated cells.
You used to be communities;
now you have clean water.

17 June - 21 June 1988

Bound

Edwin Segal

My father was a wandering
Aramian who sought my life.
As well, he was the desert chief
Who birthed me with a covenant.

Words carved on parchment echo endless
repetitions, and still I worry
at this paradox without answer,
While time's winds whip through the door of myth.

Born of my mother's ageing laughter,
swaddled in history's purple fringes,
suckled by my father's holy contract,
I am yet bound to my beginnings.

Blue thread binds me to the altar
of my father's faith; an ancient
horn locks my fate to his, and thus
have we wandered alone through time.

And time has grown, while I stand between
generations, bound to first and last.
I am my sire and seek my son's life
with understanding as deep as his.

10 January - 12 January 86.

Under the Kachere Tree
15 February to 15 March 1986
Edwin Segal

The branches spread their mythic shade and
In the cool of this place that never was
(And always is), we wait to receive
The wisdom of age, which calms our fevered
Search for the unity in our lives,
That brings order to our dry houses and
Brand new clothes, that makes us loyal to
New traditions of peaceful coexistence.
We are all one here, disciplined by
Obedience to the straits of our lives.
And as we wait, the shadow grows to
Hide the sun, and on shrine has no

Priestess and no serpent to bring good
Fortune to our lives, blotted out by
The wisdom of an age that will not
End, though its time left us yesterday.

Malawi 1992
2 August 92
Edwin Segal

Dispossessed by drought,
we drift through the heat,
across a land misted, brown
and charred by burning grass.
Smoke plumes stand across
the horizon and cooling
winds cut the land from our feet.

Immortal Diamond
(Jack Mapanje, detained 25 September, 1987)
Landeg White

Outside the bar, night, bullfrogs promising rain,
the sky a dome of stars ripped
by the black edge of the mountain.

Bloated face, trunk like a baobab,
"We've got your lame friend",
from the unmarked jeep

boasting Special Branch. Words hidden
a hemisphere off grudge
"Now you're on your own",

and I can smell here the Carlsberg
on his breath. He leers
from the smuggled page.

Lame: alone: "we're
preparing a place for him."
This clown knows the power

of pauses, the ecstasy of rhythm.
His threat is accurately
their dread. For Jack, our dear friend's poems

are out, unparoled, his metaphors dancing from lip
to lip and no heavyweight

knuckles ripping
pages can stop them.
The crippled swagger

"We've got your friend,"
calms outrage
at that night, that frog-loud prison yard, leaned

on by the mountain, where Jack, joke, patch
matchwood, hardens
like starlight, needing no crutch.

Season of Goodwill

Landeg White

Poor Ronnie who's really very liberal
Insisted when he first came out here
He didn't need a houseboy. But washing
His own shirts was a bit a of a nuisance,
So when Goodwill knelt on his doorstep,
And refused to move for two whole days,
He thought he'd give the chap a try.
Well, you can imagine what it was like
After starting like that. The fellow
Practically ruled his life. Ronnie
Couldn't pee without this character
Flushing it first and cleaning up afterwards,
And if ever he wanted a quick lunch
To get back to the office, there was
So much fuss about "wanting to prease Bwana"
That in the end he decided to sack him
And send his shirts next door. But Ronnie's
Really very liberal, and when he found
The poor bastard helping himself
To chicken bones from the dustbin
and half a stale loaf he'd chucked away,
He just couldn't bring himself to do it.
Well, you can guess what happened next.
These fellows always know when they're
On to a good thing. First it was soap.
Then there was this bag of mealie
Going cheap and could he borrow five pounds.
Then one of his wives was sick. Then it was
School fees for his children and, well,
You know how liberal poor Ronnie is.
The last straw was when he found him
Entertaining some creature he called
His uncle with imported beer straight
From the fridge! Ronnie came right over
To ask us what he should do. Well, I
Typed a letter giving the fellow notice

And made Ronnie sign it on the spot.
Of course, when Goodwill got the letter,
Ronnie had to read it to him, and he'd
Have looked bloody silly backing out.
I think Ronnie'll settle down all right.
He's got a new chap now we found for him.
You have to learn to take a firm line
With Africans or they just don't respect you.'

Notes on the Contributors

Hoffman Aipira is a Malawian Ph.D. student at the University of York in the United Kingdom.

Kisa Amateshe started teaching at High School level in June 1975. He was Head of English for several years. He has wide experience in the teaching of language and literature. He has been teaching literature and theatre arts in Kenyatta university, Nairobi (Kenya) since April, 1982. He has traveled widely. An accomplished dramatist, educationist and published poet who has facilitated at numerous workshops both in Kenya and internationally. He has also been an ardent promoter of creative writing and critical thinking.

Innocent Banda is a Malawian linguist and poet who is now resident in the United States of America. He was one od the contributors to *The Haunting Wind,* an anthology of Malawian poetry edited by Anthony Nazombe and published by Dzuka in 1990.

Sai Bwanali graduated some time ago from Chancellor College, University of Malawi.

Steve Chimombo recently retired as Professor of English at Chancellor College. He publishes WASI, a magazine for the arts in Malawi.

Arguably the most prolific Malawian poet, Frank Chipasula has spent a large part of his life in exile in Zambia and in the United States of America. He teaches literature at the University of Nebraska.

The late Zangaphee Chizeze was a lawyer.

S.E. Chiziwa is a graduate of Chancellor College, University of Malawi.

Catherine Duclos is an American citizen who has been to Malawi.

Dunstan Gausi is an officer in the Malawi Defence Force.

Cecilia Hasha is a graduate of Chancellor College, Zomba.

Maxford Iphani is Senior Education Materials Editor at the Malawi Institute of Education, Domasi, Zomba. He is one of the three editors of *The an Unsung Song: An Anthology of Malawi's on Writing in English.*

Gustave Kaliwo is a lawyer in Blantyre, Malawi.

David Kerr is a Professor in Theatre Arts at Chancellor College, University of Malawi, Zomba.

The late Kapwepwe Khonje was an Assistant Lecturer in the Department of English at Chancellor College, University of Malawi, Zomba.

Monica Brenda Kumwenda is a student at Chancellor College, Zomba.

Ken Lipenga is a Cabinet Minister. He is the author of *Waiting for a Turn* a collection of short stories published by Popular Publications in Limbe, Malawi.

John Lwanda is a Malawian medical doctor and writer who lives and works in Glasgow, Scotland, United Kingdom.

Probably the best known Malawian poet, Jack Mapanje lives with his family in the United Kingdom. He is the author of three books of verse, namely *Of Chameleons and Gods*, *The Chattering Wagtails of Mikuyu Prison* and *Skipping Without Ropes*.

Zeleza Manda teaches at the Malawi Institute of Journalism in Blantyre, Malawi.

Alfred Matiki is a Malawian linguist teaching at the University of Botswana, Gaborone Campus.

Zondiwe Mbano is an Assistant Lecturer in Language and Communication Skills at Chancellor College, University of Malawi. His poetry appeared in *The Fate of Vultures*, *The Haunting Wind* and *The Unsung Song*.

Rowland Mbvundula is a graduate of Chancellor College, University of Malawi.

M. Mkandawire is a one time member of the Chancellor College Writers' Workshop in Zomba, Malawi.

Felix Mnthali is a Professor of English at the University of Botswana. He is the author of *When Sunset Comes to Sapitwa*, a collection of poems published by NECZAM in Lusaka Zambia, in 1980.

Bright Molande is a lecturer in English literature in the Department of English at Chancellor College, University of Malawi, in Zomba. He holds a Masters in Postcolonial Studies from the University of Essex. Currently he is head of the Department of English. He has written many poems but these are not known yet because they are not published, except one or two on the internet. The poem included in this anthology could perhaps be his first significant publication.

Francis Moto, a linguist, is Principal of Chancellor College, University of Malawi. He is the author of *Gazing at the Setting Sun*, a collection of poems.

Lupenga Mphande is a Malawian poet and linguist resident in the United States of America. He teaches at Ohio State University. He has written *Crackle at Midnight*, a selection of verse published by Heinemann, Nigeria.

The late Edison Mpina was a prominent Malawian poet whose work appeared in *Summer Fires* and *The Haunting Wind*.

J.J. Msosa is a special contributor to this volume.

Khumbula Munthali is a lady writer who graduated from Chancellor College, the University of Malawi, in the eighties.

Ian Musowa was for some time a member of the Chancellor College Writers' Workshop in Zomba, Malawi.

Sam Raiti Mtamba, a graduate of the University of Malawi, now lives and works in Zimbabwe. Some of his poems appeared in *The Haunting Wind*.

Geoff Mwanja ia an established Malawian poet. Some of his poems appeared in *The Haunting Wind*.

Anthony Nazombe is an Associate Professor of English at Chancellor College, University of Malawi. His poems have been included in the following anthologies: *The Haunting Wing*, *New Accents One*, *Them/Us* and *The Unsung Song*.

Alfred Tyson Nkhoma is a former member of the Chancellor College Writers' Workshop in Zomba, Malawi.

Emmanuel Bofomo Nyirenda, another graduate of the University of Malawi, now teaches in secondary school. He has gone into self publishing.

Patrick O'Malley, an Irish priest, once lectured in the Department of English at Chancellor College, University of Malawi. He is the author of a memoir entitled *Living Dangerously*.

Niyi Osundare is an internationally recognized Nigerian poet whose only connection with the Malawian literary scene is that he wrote on Jack Mapanje's detention.

D.B.V. Phiri is a librarian at Chancellor College. His name will be familiar to readers of *The Haunting Wind*.

Kadwa Phungwako is a former member of the Chancellor College Writers' Workshop.

Ambokile Salimu is a lawyer.

A Ghanaian, Francis Sefe once taught Geography at Chancellor College. Some of his verse appeared in *The Haunting Wind*.

An American academic, Edwin Segal was at one point a Visiting Professor of Sociology at Chancellor College.

Landeg White is a widely published English writer, critic and historian. A founding member of the Chancellor College Writers' Workshop, he now lives and works in Portugal.

Glossary

Abiti	Miss, the title of an unmarried Yao woman
Akumulungu	Those who dwell with God, that is, the ancestors
Amakhosi balibale nakudhla	
Abayazi oluzayo	The Ngoni princes are engrossed in feasting; they do not realize what is coming.
Ambuye	Literally grandfather or lord.
Anankungwi	Elders who supervise initiation ceremonies. They offer advice to the initiates.
Aphungu	Representatives. For example members of parliament.
Askari	Soldiers
Awiro	Persons mourning the dead.
Baba	Father
Bandaism	The ideology propounded by Malawi's Dr. Hastings Kamuzu banda,
Boma	British Overseas Military Administration. Now used to refer to government and district administration.
Birimankhwe	Chameleon
Bwannoni	A green and fatty flying insect considered a delicacy in Malawi. Like most insects, it is drawn toward light, including street lights.
Bangwe	A board zither. It is also the name of a township in the city of Blantyre, Limbe.
Nanzikambe	Another name for the common chameleon.
Chadzunda	One of the masks involved in Gule Wamkulu, "the big dance" among the Chewa – Mang'anja of central and southern Malawi.
Chambo	A freshwater fish belonging to the Tilapia family. It is plentiful in Malawi's lakes.
Chewa	A Bantu ethnic group concentrated in the central region of Malawi; part of what historians call the Luba-Lunda migration. The language spoken by this group is called Chichewa.
Chidangwaleza	A frightening apparition; a bogey.
Chilembwe	The leader of the 1915 uprising against colonial rule in Nyasaland, now Malawi.
Chilungamo	Justices from the word kulungama, to be just or fair minded.
Chimurenga	Zimbabwe's liberation war in its various phases.
Chinangwa	Cassava

Chingwe's Hole	A hole on Zomba plateau into which, according to local tradition, the bodies of dead victims were thrown.
Chioda	A traditional dance performed by Chewa/Mang'anja/Nyanja women.
Chiperoni	A cold south easterly wind blowing over southern Malawi.
Chirundu	Originally, two fathoms of cloth sewn together by the edges and thrown round one like a 'toga', it then came to be the measure, four yards length of cloth wrapped round their waists by village women.
Chitute	A type of mouse from the word kututa meaning to collect together.
Chiuta	The Chewa/Mang'anja High God in His manifestation as the rainbow.
Chopa	A frantic Lomwe dance with no specific repertoire of songs, traditionally performed at rain-calling ceremonies or communal society prayers against pestilence. As an ethnic group, the Lomwe originated from the pres??ent day Mocambique.
Dambwe	Area in the bush or the forest where members of the Gule Wamkulu (big dance) congregate.
Ilala	The name of a vessel which sank on Lake Malawi in 30th July 1946. Currently there is Ilala II.
Imi	A Ngoni regiment.
Kachasu	A locally distilled spirit which can be dangerous to one's health. The word appears to be of Portuguese origin.
Kafula	The name of the aboriginal inhabitants of Malawi. They are also known as Abatwa. According to legend, some of them disappeared into Mulanje mountain in southern Malawi.
Kalilombe	The horned chameleon
Kalongonda	A poisonous bean boiled several times by the Lomwe people before it is consumed. It was an effective weapon against the raiding Ngoni during the nachikopa (skin or hide) war.
Kaphirintiwa	A hill in central Malawi on which, it is said, the first man and woman landed at the beginning of creation. The first part of the name simply means a low hill. Ka- is a diminutive in Chichewa.
Kavuluvulu	Whirlwind
Kwacha	It has dawned. Also the name of Malawi's currency. As a slogan it was used during the country's fight

SEASON 3 · CIVIL WAR

JERICHO™

WRITTEN BY
DAN SHOTZ, ROBERT LEVINE,
MATTHEW FEDERMAN & JASON M. BURNS

STORY BY THE JERICHO WRITING STAFF
JONATHAN E. STEINBERG, DAN SHOTZ,
CAROL BARBEE, JOSH SCHAER, MATTHEW FEDERMAN,
STEPHEN SCAIA, ROBERT LEVINE & ROBBIE THOMPSON

DRAWN BY
MATT MERHOFF
WITH ALEJANDRO F. GIRALDO

COLORED BY
JUANMAR STUDIOS, SPACE GOAT PRODUCTIONS'
MIN WU, LISA JACKSON AND HI-FI COLOUR

LETTERED BY
CRANK!

COVERS BY
SCOTT WEST

PHOTO COVERS BY
PATRICK WYMORE AND ZAC FISHER

ORIGINAL SERIES EDITORS
CODY DeMATTEIS AND SCOTT DUNBIER

IN ASSOCIATION WITH JERICHO EXECUTIVE PRODUCERS
JON TURTELTAUB, CAROL BARBEE, KARIM ZREIK,
DAN SHOTZ & JONATHAN E. STEINBERG

COLLECTION EDITS BY
JUSTIN EISINGER AND ALONZO SIMON

COLLECTION DESIGN BY
NEIL UYETAKE

COLLECTION COVER ART BY
JASON MOORE

COLLECTION BACK COVER ART BY
MICHAEL STRIBLING

Special Thanks to Risa Kessler and John Van Citters at CBS Consumer Products

ISBN: 978-1-60010-939-3

14 13 12 11   1 2 3 4

Ted Adams, CEO & Publisher
Greg Goldstein, Chief Operating Officer
Robbie Robbins, EVP/Sr. Graphic Artist
Chris Ryall, Chief Creative Officer/Editor-in-Chief
Matthew Ruzicka, CPA, Chief Financial Officer
Alan Payne, VP of Sales

Become our fan on Facebook **facebook.com/idwpublishing**
Follow us on Twitter **@idwpublishing**
Check us out on YouTube **youtube.com/idwpublishing**
www.IDWPUBLISHING.com

CHAPTER ONE

WE WERE CUT OFF.

NO POWER. NO PHONES.

GRADUALLY, WE LEARNED THE TRUTH.

TWENTY-THREE CITIES, DESTROYED BY NUCLEAR BLAST.

THE COUNTRY IN RUINS. LAW AND ORDER A THING OF THE PAST. CHAOS, JUST OVER THE HORIZON.

WASN'T LONG BEFORE IT FOUND US.

AND TOOK OUR BEST FROM US.

I KNEW IT WAS COMING.

IT WAS MY JOB TO STOP IT.

FIVE YEARS, LIVING AS SOMEONE ELSE. COUNTLESS NAMES. COUNTLESS COVERS.

I WATCHED DENVER IGNITE IN A CLOUD.

MY WIFE AND CHILDREN BESIDE ME.

AT LEAST THEY WERE SAFE.

WELCOME TO JERICHO, KANSA

FOR THE MOMENT, ANYWAY.

I'D BROUGHT SOMETHING WITH US.

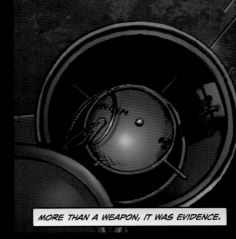

MORE THAN A WEAPON, IT WAS EVIDENCE.

PROOF OF A PLOT TO LEVEL THIS COUNTRY; REBUILD IT AS SOMETHING ELSE.

SOMETHING TERRIBLE.

THEY KILLED EVERYONE ON MY TEAM TO FIND IT. THEN THEY CAME FOR ME.

EXCEPT WHEN THEY CAME FOR ME... THEY CAME UNDER A FLAG.

THERE IS NO ALLIED STATES! CHEYENNE'S AUTHORITY IS COMPLETELY ILLEGITIMATE--

WELL, THERE'S TWENTY-ONE STATES WEST OF THE MISSISSIPPI THAT DON'T QUITE SEE IT THAT WAY.

SEEMS THEY LIKE HAVING A POWER GRID, RUNNING WATER AND A MILITARY THAT CAN STILL HOP TO.

GENTLEMEN!

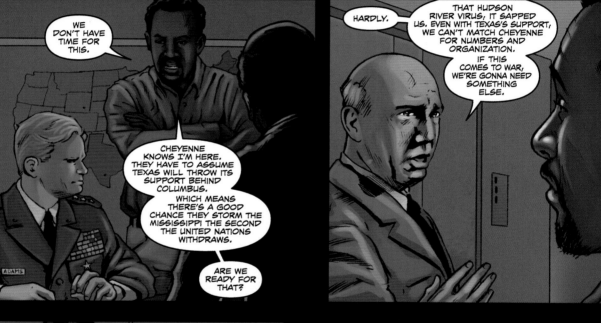

WE DON'T HAVE TIME FOR THIS.

CHEYENNE KNOWS I'M HERE. THEY HAVE TO ASSUME TEXAS WILL THROW ITS SUPPORT BEHIND COLUMBUS.

WHICH MEANS THERE'S A GOOD CHANCE THEY STORM THE MISSISSIPPI THE SECOND THE UNITED NATIONS WITHDRAWS.

ARE WE READY FOR THAT?

HARDLY.

THAT HUDSON RIVER VIRUS, IT SAPPED US. EVEN WITH TEXAS'S SUPPORT, WE CAN'T MATCH CHEYENNE FOR NUMBERS AND ORGANIZATION.

IF THIS COMES TO WAR, WE'RE GONNA NEED SOMETHING ELSE.

"SOME KIND OF X-FACTOR THAT CHEYENNE WON'T SEE COMING.

"AND FOR THE LIFE OF ME, I DON'T KNOW WHAT THAT IS."

ETA to target: 10:12

"READY JAKE?"

"RUMORS ARE THE NIGHT YOU LANDED, THEY TOOK A BOMB OFF YOUR PLANE."

"I CAN'T TALK ABOUT THAT."

"NOT TRYING TO PUT YOU ON THE SPOT. IT'S JUST, PEOPLE ARE SAYING IT WAS THE SAME KIND OF BOMB THAT BLEW UP ALL OUR CITIES. A NUKE.

"IS THAT TRUE?"

SO ALL THAT STUFF ABOUT THE BOMBS BEING FROM NORTH KOREA, THAT WAS A LIE?

"IT'S WHY THOSE PLANES WERE CHASING US. CHEYENNE DOESN'T WANT ANYONE TO KNOW WHERE THE BOMBS WERE MADE."

"YOU MEAN THEY'RE HOMEMADE?

"JESUS, YOU'RE SAYING AMERICANS WERE BEHIND THE ATTACKS."

"ONE AMERICAN... JOHN SMITH."

"STRATEGIC SITES WITHIN SAN ANTONIO WERE ALSO DESTROYED.

"CIVILIAN CASUALTY RATES WILL BE HIGH...

"...BUT ACCEPTABLE.

KRA-KOOOM

WANTED
BY THE ASA
ACTS OF TERRORISM

Jake Green   Robert Hawkins

Any Cooperation with these Terrorists is a Federal Crime.

If you have any information about these persons, contact your local ASA office or nearest ASA Embassy or Consulate.

WHAT'S THIS?

IT'S FROM THE MAJOR.

"—BUT THEY'RE NOT COMING HOME."

HAWKINS, TALK TO ME.

WHERE ARE WE GOING?

NEW MEXICO.

SURE I DON'T HAVE TO TELL YOU THAT'S CHEYENNE TERRITORY.

NO CHOICE.

WHAT IS THIS?

Help me.

A MESSAGE. FROM JOHN SMITH.

"I DON'T GET IT. WHY WOULD SMITH WANT YOUR HELP?"

"MY GUESS IS HE GOT CAPTURED AFTER YOU SHOT HIM IN CHEYENNE. HE WANTS US TO BREAK HIM OUT."

"HAWKINS, THAT'S CRAZY."

Loomer Ridge Prison
ASA Property
Trespassers will be shot on sight

"THINK ABOUT IT, JAKE. WITH TEXAS OUT OF THE PICTURE, THE EAST CANNOT DEFEAT CHEYENNE HEAD-ON. WE'RE GONNA HAVE TO WIN THIS WAR SOME OTHER WAY."

BEFORE HE TURNED ON CHEYENNE, SMITH HELPED BUILD THE MONSTER. NO ONE KNOWS THEIR SYSTEM BETTER THAN HIM. WHICH MEANS...

HE KNOWS THEIR WEAKNESSES.

"IF WE CAN GET HIM TO COLUMBUS, WE MIGHT JUST GET A LOOK AT WHAT'S INSIDE HIS HEAD."

"SOUNDS GOOD. MY ONLY CONCERN IS...

"...HOW DO WE FIND HIM?"

"RELAX, JAKE...

CHAPTER TWO

"WELCOME TO THE OPEN PLAINS REFUGEE CENTER. HOW ARE YOU THIS MORNING?"

REFUGEE INTAKE STATION
PLEASE HAVE ID READY

WE HAVE EVERYTHING YOU NEED DURING YOUR PROCESSING PERIOD. FOOD, SUPPLIES AND SHELTER.

MOST IMPORTANTLY, WE CAN HELP YOU FIND YOUR LOVED ONES WHEN YOU REGISTER.

NAME?

FINE.

WONDERFUL... HERE'S YOUR TEMPORARY PASS.

WE'LL JUST NEED TO TAKE YOUR PHOTOGRAPH FOR SECURITY REASONS.

PLEASE STEP TO THE LEFT.

MIKE... JOHNSTON.

UM... WE'RE WANTED MEN.

AREN'T THOSE PHOTOS GONNA BE A PROBLEM?

THEY'RE GONNA LAND ON A DESK WITH A THOUSAND OTHER PHOTOS.

FIGURE WE GET AT LEAST A FEW HOURS BEFORE SOMEONE PICKS THEM OUT OF THE PILE.

"WHAT IS IT WE'RE LOOKING AT, MAJOR?"

WANTED BY THE ASA HEROES

Jake Green

Robert Hawkins

Any Cooperation with these Terrorists is a Federal Crime.

you have any information about th...
...rsons, contact your loc...
nearest ASA Embassy o...

BAILEY'S TAVERN

THIS MAP SHOWS THE AREAS OF OPERATION FOR ALL THE ASA MILITARY DIVISIONS STATIONED IN AND AROUND KANSAS.

GREEN INDICATES UNITS WHOSE COMMANDERS I'VE PERSUADED TO NO LONGER SUPPORT PRESIDENT TOMARCHIO.

THEY'RE STAYING AT THEIR POSTS, CONTINUING TO TAKE ORDERS FROM CHEYENNE UNTIL I GIVE THE GREEN LIGHT.

AND THE RED?

THOSE ARE THE REST. THE LOYALISTS WHO STILL ANSWER TO CHEYENNE. IF WE'RE HOPING TO BLOODLESSLY SEIZE POWER BACK FROM TOMARCHIO, I'M GONNA NEED A LOT MORE OF THEM IN MY CAMP.

I'M IMPRESSED YOU'VE MANAGED TO TURN AS MANY OF THEM AS YOU HAVE...

...GIVEN WHAT'S AT RISK FOR YOU.

FORTUNATELY, THE EVIDENCE ON ROBERT HAWKINS' LAPTOP IS SO COMPELLING.

THESE OFFICERS ARE HONORABLE MEN.

ONCE THEY'VE LEARNED THAT THEIR LEADERS COVERED UP THE TRUTH ABOUT THE ATTACKS IN ORDER TO SEIZE POWER, IT'S IMPOSSIBLE FOR THEM TO MAINTAIN THEIR ALLEGIANCE.

DON'T TREAD ON ME

SO YOU'VE BEEN AT THIS FOR A WHILE...

IT'S NOT JUST MY LIFE THAT'S AT RISK. IT'S THE LIVES OF EACH OF MY MEN. BUT I DON'T HAVE A CHOICE.

"...IS THERE A REASON YOU'RE LETTING US IN NOW?"

"ONE OF THE REMAINING LOYALISTS, A MAJOR DOMINICK PETRELLA, IS DUE IN JERICHO THIS AFTERNOON.

"PETRELLA IS HIGHLY RESPECTED AMONG THE A.S.A. BRASS.

"HE'S ALSO ADORED BY HIS MEN.

"EARNING HIS ALLEGIANCE WOULD BE A GAME-CHANGER.

"OFFICIALLY, HE'S HERE TO LEARN MY PACIFICATION STRATEGIES. 'QUELLING' THE JERICHO UPRISING HAS EARNED ME A REPUTATION AS AN EXPERT COUNTERINSURGENT.

"AS THE LEADERS OF THE JERICHO UNDERGROUND, I NEED YOU TO SPREAD THE WORD TO YOUR PEOPLE. BE MINDFUL. STAY ON YOUR BEST BEHAVIOR. ANY HINT OF REBELLION...

...AND WE COULD LOSE HIM.

HOW OLD ARE YOU, DALE?

SEVENTEEN.

AND YOUR STORE IS THE REGION'S PRIMARY SOURCE FOR FOOD AND SUPPLIES.

YOUR ORGANIZATION, YOUR CONNECTIONS, ARE KEY TO KEEPING ORDER IN THIS AREA.

LOT OF RESPONSIBILITY FOR SOMEONE YOUR AGE. SURE YOU HAD PLENTY OF OPPORTUNITY TO SELL TO JENNINGS AND RALL. WHY DIDN'T YOU?

NOT MY CHOICE TO MAKE.

GRACIE LEIGH. SHE STOOD UP TO A ROAD GANG, WAS KILLED FOR IT. THEN YOU INHERITED THE STORE. CORRECT?

AND HOW HAVE YOU DEALT WITH THE ROAD GANG ISSUE? FROM WHAT I HEAR, YOUR SHIPMENTS GO LARGELY UNTOUCHED. IN FACT—

—THERE DOESN'T SEEM TO BE ANY CHECK ON YOUR POWERS, FROM EITHER SIDE OF THE LAW.

I HAVE TO ADMIT, I FIND THAT DISTURBING. SEEMS LIKE A RECIPE FOR TROUBLE.

CORRECT.

NO TROUBLE HERE.

HE'S BEEN IN THERE A WHILE.

IS THAT GOOD OR BAD?

TWO HOURS.

MAJOR BECK--

I'LL... HAVE TO BE GOING NOW. YOU'VE GIVEN ME A LOT TO THINK ABOUT ON THE RIDE HOME.

MAJOR... MIGHT I SUGGEST THAT YOU AND YOUR MEN STAY IN JERICHO FOR THE NIGHT? I'D REST EASIER KNOWING YOU WERE TRAVELING IN THE MORNING...

I APPRECIATE THE OFFER, BUT I'M EXPECTED AT MY POST. DON'T WORRY... I'LL BE IN TOUCH VERY SOON.

DID IT WORK, HEATHER? IS HE WITH US?

HE DIDN'T SAY.

VERY GOOD THEN.

THERE'S NO WAY TO KNOW.

I GUESS WE'LL FIND OUT SOON ENOUGH.

JERICHO

..-..-.'...'/...:'...'/-..../'.-.'-

CHAPTER THREE

DALE!

I MISSED YOU SO MUCH!

ME, TOO, SKYLAR.

I'M SO SORRY ABOUT YOUR PARENTS...

I HAD TO TRY LOOKING, YOU KNOW? TRACKED THEM TO JUST NORTH OF MANHATTAN AND THEN NOTHING... THE HUDSON VIRUS TOOK OUT SO MANY PEOPLE...

BUT I MADE A GREAT DEAL FOR SOME MEDICAL SUPPLIES.

OH YEAH?

THEY'LL BE HERE BY THE END OF THE WEEK. WE CAN MARK THEM UP HUGE AND STILL COME IN WAY UNDER WHAT J&R IS CHARGING...

THAT'S GREAT.

"DID I MISS ANYTHING WHILE I WAS GONE?"

NO. BEEN PRETTY QUIET AROUND HERE.

I DON'T SEE HIM.

THERE HE IS.

HELLO, BEAUTIFUL...

I'M SO *HAPPY* YOU'RE HERE.

AND WHO'S THIS RUNT YOU GOT WITH YOU?

GLAD YOU COULD MAKE IT, UNCLE EMMETT.

WOULDN'T MISS IT FOR THE WORLD. YOU KNOW THAT.

TRIP GO SMOOTHLY?

SURE. IF YOU DON'T COUNT GETTING STOPPED AT AN A.S.A. CHECKPOINT EVERY TEN MILES.

THINGS STILL BAD BACK EAST?

I SUPPOSE YOU COULD SAY THAT. THEN AGAIN...

IT IS STILL A FREE COUNTRY.

"I NOW PRONOUNCE YOU MAN AND WIFE..."

BZZZZZZZ

GO AHEAD.

SHIFT CHANGE, BUDDY. MIND BUZZING ME IN, CARD READER'S NOT WORKING...

YOU'RE EARLY...

OUGHTTA BE HEARING ALARMS BY NOW.

MMMMPPH!

NOT YET...

RARARRARARARAK

...NOW.

OFF BY A MILLISECOND. YOU MUST BE SLIPPING.

THAT MEANS WE'RE LOOKING AT AN EXTRA CHOKE POINT. WE SHOULD GET MOVING.

EVERYBODY...

SMITH'S OUT OF HIS CELL. THEY'VE GOT HIM IN THE INTERROGATION WING.

RARARRARARARARA

WHO WANTS ANOTHER COCKTAIL?

CLUB SODA FOR ME...

YOU CAN'T SERIOUSLY BELIEVE THAT?

I WOULDN'T HAVE SAID IT IF I DIDN'T. THE A.S.A. KEEPS US FED, KEEPS US SAFE... BETTER THAN WHAT YOU HAVE OVER IN THE EAST. EVERYONE DYING FROM A VIRUS, NO INFRASTRUCTURE...

I LOOK AROUND HERE, ALL I SEE IS A BUNCH OF SCARED CHILDREN, LOOKING TO DADDY TO MAKE EVERYTHING BETTER. AS IF THEY'VE FORGOTTEN HOW THIS COUNTRY CAME TO BE IN THE FIRST PLACE...

THAT'S THE PROBLEM, MAYOR. I DON'T THINK WE HAVE A WHOLE LOT OF TIME LEFT.

CLINK CLINK

BUT YOU KNOW WHAT WE DO HAVE? A CONSTITUTION.

A FRAMEWORK FOR A GOVERNMENT THAT ENSURES OUR FREEDOM ABOVE ALL ELSE

YOU'RE TALKING ABOUT WAR, EMMETT? IS THAT WHAT YOU'RE ADVOCATING?

THIS ISN'T THE PLACE FOR THIS, GUYS. SAVE IT FOR ANOTHER TIME.

THERE'S THE DOOR.

ON MY MARK...

YOU GOT MY MESSAGE...

CHAPTER FOUR

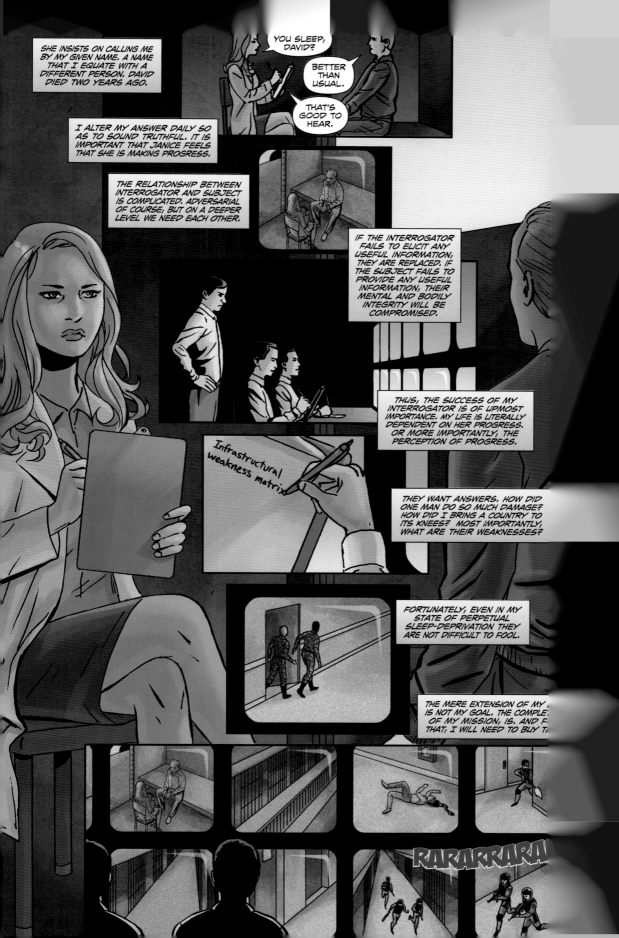

FROM THE SKY IT LOOKS EXACTLY LIKE THE SCALE MODEL–TIDY, EFFICIENT... A PROJECTION OF AMERICAN ORDER ON AN ALIEN LANDSCAPE.

FORWARD DEPLOYMENT BASE RB–362, AFGHANISTAN.

JENNINGS & RALL

IN-COUNTRY THEY CALLED IT "CAMP CUSTER." A GYM, CHURCH, MOVIE THEATER, EVEN A PIZZA PLACE. ALL OF THE COMFORTS OF HOME. SO MODERN AND "SAFE" THEY TOLD ME I COULD BRING MY WIFE...

PEOPLE ARE ENDLESSLY ADAPTABLE. WHEREVER THEY FIND THEMSELVES THEY WILL CREATE A HOME, A SENSE OF NORMALCY, A FEELING OF SAFETY. EVEN IF IT IS AN ILLUSION.

BUT EXTREME AND CONSTANT STRESS WILL WARP THIS INSTINCT. CHAOS WILL BECOME HOME. FEAR IS NORMALCY. ANGER IS SAFETY. PEACE IS THE ILLUSION.

POST-TRAUMATIC STRESS DISORDER...

RAMPANT DRUG ABUSE.

BINGE DRINKING.

VIOLENT OFF-DUTY BEHAVIOR.

WHOEVER HAD WRITTEN THE PREVIOUS REPORT WAS WILLFULLY BLIND OR LYING ABOUT THE CONDITIONS ON THE GROUND. I REVISED THE DATA. AND I GROUNDED AN ENTIRE PLATOON IN THE FIRST WEEK...

ADMINISTRATIVE LEAVE

...WHAT I FAILED TO ACCOUNT FOR WAS THE DIFFERENCE BETWEEN SOLDIERS AND MERCENARIES. SOLDIERS ARE HAPPY TO BE OUT OF HARM'S WAY. MERCENARIES NEED THE PAYCHECK.

CRAACK

MY ONLY CONSOLATION IS MY MEMORIES OF THE ATTACK ARE BRIEF.

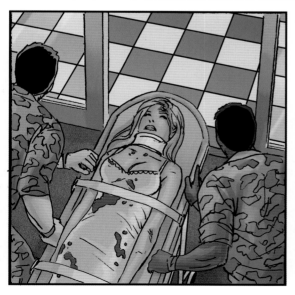

A LIFE IS A WORLD UNTO ITSELF. ITS OWN BEGINNING. ITS OWN ENDING. EVERY DEATH IS ITS OWN APOCALYPSE.

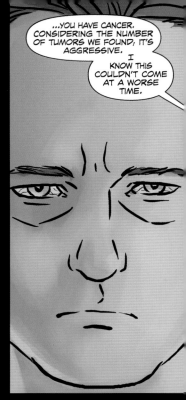

...YOU HAVE CANCER. CONSIDERING THE NUMBER OF TUMORS WE FOUND, IT'S AGGRESSIVE. I KNOW THIS COULDN'T COME AT A WORSE TIME.

BUT... I HAVE SOME MORE BAD NEWS.

I SAW SOME THINGS I DIDN'T LIKE IN YOUR X-RAY, HAD THEM DO FOLLOW UP TESTS. IT CONFIRMED MY FEARS...

I KNOW YOU'VE SUFFERED A TERRIBLE LOSS.

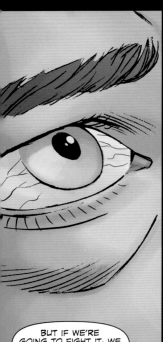

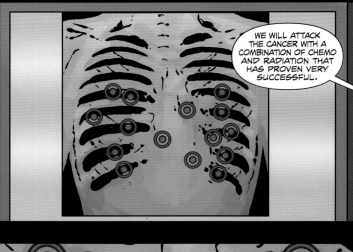

WE WILL ATTACK THE CANCER WITH A COMBINATION OF CHEMO AND RADIATION THAT HAS PROVEN VERY SUCCESSFUL.

IT WILL KILL THE HEALTHY CELLS ALONG WITH THE CANCER CELLS.

BUT WITH SWIFT ACTION, AND WITH ANY LUCK, WE CAN DESTROY THE CANCER COMPLETELY AND LET THE HEALTHY CELLS REBUILD.

BUT IF WE'RE GOING TO FIGHT IT, WE NEED TO BE JUST AS AGGRESSIVE. WE'RE FLYING YOU BACK TO AMERICA TONIGHT.

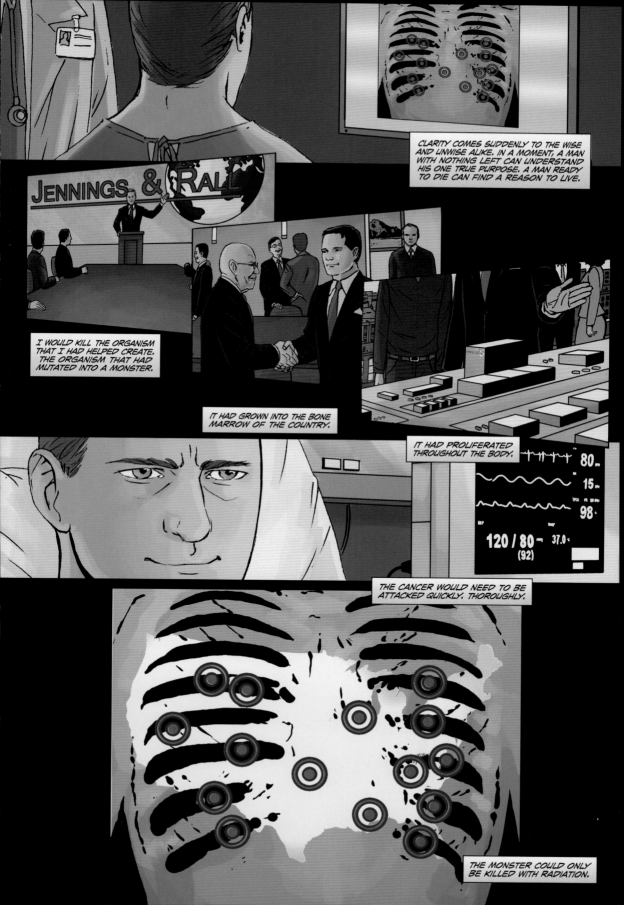

CLARITY COMES SUDDENLY TO THE WISE AND UNWISE ALIKE. IN A MOMENT, A MAN WITH NOTHING LEFT CAN UNDERSTAND HIS ONE TRUE PURPOSE. A MAN READY TO DIE CAN FIND A REASON TO LIVE.

JENNINGS & RALL

I WOULD KILL THE ORGANISM THAT I HAD HELPED CREATE. THE ORGANISM THAT HAD MUTATED INTO A MONSTER.

IT HAD GROWN INTO THE BONE MARROW OF THE COUNTRY.

IT HAD PROLIFERATED THROUGHOUT THE BODY.

80
15
98
120 / 80
(92)
37.0

THE CANCER WOULD NEED TO BE ATTACKED QUICKLY. THOROUGHLY.

THE MONSTER COULD ONLY BE KILLED WITH RADIATION.

I NEVER SUBMITTED MY RESIGNATION. I NEVER LET THE COMPANY KNOW THAT I WAS ON MY WAY BACK TO THE STATES. I NEVER LET THEM SEE ME COMING.

DAVID, YOU'RE BACK.

MY SECURITY PERMISSIONS WERE TURNED OFF. YOUR IDEA, NOW THAT YOU HAVE MOVED INTO MY OFFICE?

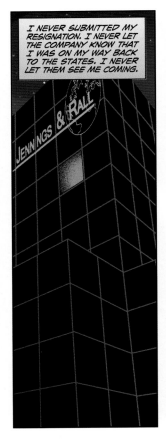

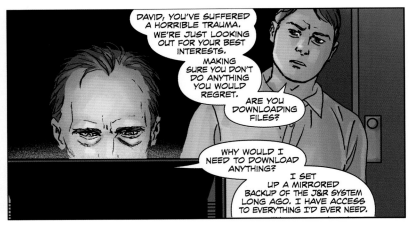

DAVID, YOU'VE SUFFERED A HORRIBLE TRAUMA. WE'RE JUST LOOKING OUT FOR YOUR BEST INTERESTS.

MAKING SURE YOU DON'T DO ANYTHING YOU WOULD REGRET.

ARE YOU DOWNLOADING FILES?

WHY WOULD I NEED TO DOWNLOAD ANYTHING?

I SET UP A MIRRORED BACKUP OF THE J&R SYSTEM LONG AGO. I HAVE ACCESS TO EVERYTHING I'D EVER NEED.

DID YOU KNOW THAT JENNINGS AND RALL HAS BUILT AND ABANDONED EIGHT HARDENED FALL-OUT SHELTERS WITH COMMAND AND CONTROL CAPACITY OVER THE LAST TWENTY YEARS?

THE HIGHER-UPS ALWAYS LOST INTEREST AS SOMETHING NEWER AND SHINIER CAME ALONG.

BUT I MADE CERTAIN THAT EACH SITE WAS MAINTAINED JUST IN CASE.

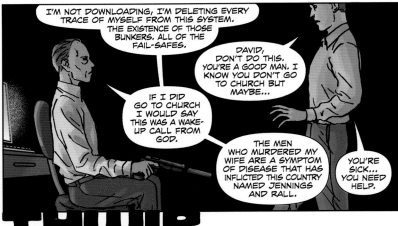

I'M NOT DOWNLOADING, I'M DELETING EVERY TRACE OF MYSELF FROM THIS SYSTEM. THE EXISTENCE OF THOSE BUNKERS. ALL OF THE FAIL-SAFES.

DAVID, DON'T DO THIS. YOU'RE A GOOD MAN. I KNOW YOU DON'T GO TO CHURCH BUT MAYBE...

IF I DID GO TO CHURCH I WOULD SAY THIS WAS A WAKE-UP CALL FROM GOD.

THE MEN WHO MURDERED MY WIFE ARE A SYMPTOM OF DISEASE THAT HAS INFLICTED THIS COUNTRY NAMED JENNINGS AND RALL.

YOU'RE SICK... YOU NEED HELP.

THWIP

THE WHOLE COUNTRY IS SICK.

I AM THE ONLY ONE WHO CAN CURE IT.

AFTER THE FALL OF THE SOVIET EMPIRE, THE COLLECTION OF LOOSE NUCLEAR MATERIAL BECAME A PRIORITY. THE OPERATION FOR THIS COLLECTION WAS CALLED "RED BELL."

THE MATERIAL WOULD BE BROUGHT TO AMERICA AND STORED FOR SAFE KEEPING.

THIS WAS MEANT TO BE THE JOB OF THE MILITARY, BUT WITHOUT THE KNOWLEDGE OR CONSENT OF CONGRESS, JENNINGS AND RALL HAD OVERTAKEN THESE RESPONSIBILITIES.

AND ANYTHING THAT J&R COULD TOUCH, I COULD TOUCH.

THAT'S ALL OF THEM.

I KNOW I'M NOT SUPPOSED TO ASK BUT USUALLY I DELIVER THIS STUFF TO OAK RIDGE.

WHY HERE?

THWIP

YOU'RE RIGHT.

YOU'RE NOT SUPPOSED TO ASK.

THOSE DEEMED CAPABLE OF CARRYING OUT THEIR MISSION RECEIVED A PHONE.

I RATED FRINGE GROUPS ON SEVERAL CRITERIA: POTENTIAL FOR VIOLENCE, OPERATIVE INFRASTRUCTURE, GROUP COHESION AND EFFECTIVE LEADERSHIP.

I KNOW WHO YOU ARE. I KNOW WHAT YOU ARE TRYING TO DO. AND I WANT TO HELP.

WHO IS THIS?

...CALL ME JOHN SMITH.

EACH GROUP WAS GIVEN SPECIFIC INSTRUCTIONS TO RECEIVE A PACKAGE DROP. INSIDE THE PACKAGE WAS A SMOKE BOMB. HARMLESS. NOT ENOUGH TO DRAW ATTENTION FROM LAW ENFORCEMENT AGENCIES.

THE RUN-THROUGH WAS SUCCESSFUL. TIMED PERFECTLY. EACH GROUP UNDERSTOOD THE PACKAGE TO BE A BOMB THAT WOULD TAKE LIVES AND EACH FOLLOWED THROUGH WITH THE PLAN. AS PER INSTRUCTIONS, NO ONE LOOKED INSIDE THEIR PACKAGE.

NEXT TIME, THE PACKAGE WOULD BE LARGER.

I WAS NOT IN THE MEETING WHEN DIRECTOR VALENTE AND SENATOR TOMARCHIO WERE INFORMED THAT AN ENTIRE SHIPMENT OF NUCLEAR MATERIAL HAD DISAPPEARED ON J&R'S WATCH.

HE KNOWS EVERYTHING ABOUT OUR SYSTEM...

HE HAS AN AXE TO GRIND AND HE HAS COMPLETELY DISAPPEARED OFF THE GRID.

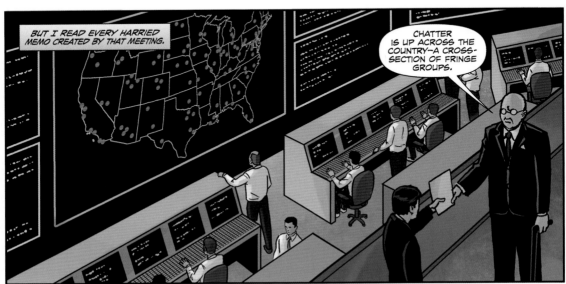

BUT I READ EVERY HARRIED MEMO CREATED BY THAT MEETING.

CHATTER IS UP ACROSS THE COUNTRY—A CROSS-SECTION OF FRINGE GROUPS.

IF EVEN ONE OF THOSE BOMBS DETONATES, HOW LONG UNTIL THEY TRACE IT BACK TO J&R?

USING THEM FOR OPERATION RED BELL WAS TECHNICALLY ILLEGAL.

WE'RE ON THE HOOK FOR EVERYTHING. THIS GOES BEYOND LOSING OUR JOBS, TOM, WE'RE TALKING ABOUT PRISON.

THEIR FIRST CONCERN WAS NOT THE COUNTRY BUT THEMSELVES.

IT WILL NEVER GET THAT FAR. I'LL PUT OUR BEST PEOPLE ON IT.

THEY'LL FIND THOSE BOMBS, TAKE DOWN THOSE CELLS. NO ONE WILL EVER KNOW.

VALENTE BROUGHT TOGETHER AN OFF-THE-BOOKS TEAM TO CLEAN UP HIS MESS. THEY ALREADY KNEW MUCH ABOUT MY PLAN, BASED ON THE REPORT I WROTE IN NINETEEN-NINETY-THREE. MY ONE ALTERATION: ST. LOUIS WAS SWAPPED OUT FOR CHEYENNE ON THE TARGET LIST.

HOW DO THEY KNOW THE HEAD OF THIS THING IS AN AMERICAN?

YOU GET THE FEELING THAT THEY'RE NOT TELLING US EVERYTHING?

JUST WHAT WE NEED TO KNOW, LIKE ALWAYS, DOESN'T CHANGE THE JOB ANY, RIGHT?

I DON'T KNOW... THIS TIME IT FEELS DIFFERENT.

VALENTE KNEW IT ALL—THE WRONGDOINGS OF J&R, THEIR CORRUPT RELATIONSHIP WITH THE GOVERNMENT, THE FACT THAT ONE OF THEIR FORMER EXECUTIVES WAS PLOTTING A MASSIVE TERRORIST ATTACK.

BUT HE CHOSE TO HOLD BACK INTEL FROM HIS OWN TEAM, TO TIE THEIR HANDS, RATHER THAN RISK EXPOSURE AND SCANDAL.

THE SECOND AMERICAN REVOLUTION STARTS HERE!

ONLY ONE PERSON ON VALENTE'S TEAM CONCERNED ME. A MAN NAMED ROBERT HAWKINS.

HAWKINS, ROBERT

THROUGH J&R I HAD ACCESS TO ALL OF HIS CONFIDENTIAL DATA.

I WATCHED HIS FAMILY FALL APART WHILE HE HUNTED ME. I HAD TO RESPECT HIS DUTY; HIS DETERMINATION; I BEGAN TO REGARD HIM AS A POTENTIAL ALLY. IN THE WORLD TO COME I WOULD NEED ALL OF THE ALLIES I COULD FIND.

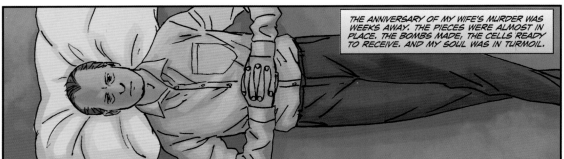

THE ANNIVERSARY OF MY WIFE'S MURDER WAS WEEKS AWAY. THE PIECES WERE ALMOST IN PLACE. THE BOMBS MADE, THE CELLS READY TO RECEIVE. AND MY SOUL WAS IN TURMOIL.

HOW MANY INNOCENTS WOULD DIE BY MY HAND? WAS I INSANE? WOULD THE WORLD BE REMADE ANEW, CLEANSED BY FIRE? OR WOULD I ONLY MAKE MY ENEMY STRONGER?

WOULD SHE BE ASHAMED OF ME? WAS IT TOO LATE TO BACK OUT?

CLICK

IT'S NOT TOO LATE.

ONE CALL TO HAWKINS, I COULD END THIS. I COULD TESTIFY TO THE SINS OF J&R BOTH HERE AND ABROAD. OR I COULD DISAPPEAR FOREVER.

BUT THEN I SAW THE FILE FOR PROJECT BOXCAR. DISSEMINATED FROM J&R TO SELECT FIGURES IN THE HIGHEST LEVELS OF GOVERNMENT, EYES ONLY.

THE GOAL OF BOXCAR WAS TO BURY THE KNOWLEDGE OF MY EXISTENCE; OF THE CONNECTION BETWEEN J&R AND THE MISSING NUCLEAR MATERIAL.

THE ATTACKS HAD YET TO HAPPEN BUT THE COVER-UP HAD ALREADY BEGUN. I REALIZED THEN THAT I HAD ALWAYS EXPECTED THEM TO STOP ME AT THE COST OF REVEALING THEIR OWN COMPLICITY, THEIR CORRUPTION. BUT IT WAS A COST THEY WERE UNWILLING TO PAY.

I AM MOVING UP THE TIMETABLE.

GET READY.

I COULD NOT RISK FURTHER DOUBT. IT WAS CLEAR TO ME NOW THAT I HAD NO CHOICE. INSANITY WOULD BE ALLOWING SUCH MEN TO STAY IN POWER. ALLOWING THE PEOPLE OF THIS COUNTRY TO REMAIN ASLEEP. I WAS ABOUT TO SOUND THE LOUDEST WAKE UP CALL IN THE HISTORY OF MANKIND.

LIKE A BLAST FROM THE HORNS OF THE ARCHANGELS.

JENNINGS & RALL

WE ALL DESERVED THIS. WE WERE ALL COMPLICIT. WE WOULD ALL PAY FOR THE MONSTER WE HAD CREATED.

THEY STOPPED THE BOMB HEADING TO NEW YORK.

ROBERT HAWKINS PREVENTED HIS BOMB FROM REACHING COLUMBUS.

A SECRET RING OF SECURITY HAD BEEN ORDERED AROUND CHEYENNE. TOMARCHIO, VALENTE AND A SHADOW GOVERNMENT HAD FALLEN BACK—HIDING OUT IN J&R BUNKERS—TO AWAIT THE COMING STORM. THE BOMB DESTINED FOR THEM WAS STOPPED AND DETONATED IN LAWRENCE, KANSAS.

IT ALL WOULD HAVE BEEN SO EASILY AVERTED IF THEY CARED ABOUT STOPPING IT MORE THAN SAVING THEIR OWN SKIN.

I FAILED TO KILL THE MONSTER...

...BUT I WILL NEVER STOP TRYING.

YOU GOT MY MESSAGE...

MY NEW ALLIES RISKED THEIR LIVES TO FREE ME.

DO YOU HAVE ANY IDEA WHAT YOU ARE DOING?

THE KIND OF MAN YOU ARE SETTING LOOSE ON THE WORLD?

BUT NOT FOR MY SAKE...

THANK YOU, CHAVEZ.

...I AM OBVIOUSLY NECESSARY FOR THEIR GOALS.

LITTLE DO THEY KNOW...

HE LOOKS LIKE HE'S OUT.

ARE YOU SURE THIS WAS A GOOD IDEA? CAN WE CONTROL HIM?

WE'RE GONNA HAVE TO. HE'S OUR ONLY SHOT TO WIN THIS WAR.

...THEY ARE ALSO NECESSARY FOR MINE.

CHAPTER FIVE

"DAVID REYNOLDS* IS FREE...

*A.K.A. JOHN SMITH

"...AND ROBERT HAWKINS HAS HIM.

"THAT'S WHAT YOU'RE TELLING ME?"

"I'M AFRAID SO, MR. PRESIDENT."

YOU ASSURED ME HAWKINS WOULDN'T BE A PROBLEM.

NOW HE'S DESTROYED OUR MOST SECURE FACILITY AND ESCAPED WITH THE MASTERMIND OF THE SEPTEMBER ATTACKS.

THE ONE MAN ALIVE WHO CAN EXPOSE EVERYTHING!

HOW DID HAWKINS EVEN KNOW WE HAD REYNOLDS?

MY GUESS WOULD BE REYNOLDS REACHED OUT FOR HELP.

MEANING WHAT? THEY'RE PARTNERS NOW?

A SAFE ASSUMPTION. THEIR INTERESTS ARE ALIGNED, AFTER ALL.

THIS IS ON YOU, THOMAS.

YOU'RE THE ONE WHO INSISTED WE KEEP REYNOLDS ALIVE. YOU THOUGHT YOU COULD BREAK HIM, AND ALL HE DID WAS STRING YOU ALONG...

...MEANWHILE, WE'RE THREE WEEKS AWAY FROM JUMPING THE MISSISSIPPI! IF HIS STORY REACHES DAYLIGHT...

HIS STORY IS IRRELEVANT. MY ONLY CONCERN IS PROTECTING OUR OPERATION. REYNOLDS IS AN ASSET. THAT'S THE ONLY REASON HAWKINS WOULD RISK FREEING HIM.

THEN MAYBE YOU CAN DO US ALL A FAVOR AND GET HIM BACK.

I'VE ENLISTED MR. PALMER HERE TO LEAD THE SEARCH.

WISE, CONSIDERING YOUR TRACK RECORD SO FAR. NOW IF THAT'S ALL, I'VE GOT AN INVASION TO SELL. GOOD DAY, GENTLEMEN.

MR. PRESIDENT.

WHERE ARE THEY?

STOPPED, FIFTY-THREE MILES FROM THE STATE LINE.

SHOULD WE APPREHEND THEM?

NOT YET...

"LADIES AND GENTLEMEN, THE PRESIDENT OF THE ALLIED STATES!"

WHAT DO YOU HAVE TO OFFER ME?

RISKY. COMING ALL THIS WAY NOT KNOWING IF I'D BE OF ANY REAL USE.

HOW CAN YOU BE SURE I WASN'T BAITING YOU?

BECAUSE YOU'RE THE ONLY PERSON IN THE WORLD WHO WANTS TO STOP JENNINGS AND RALL MORE THAN ME. YOU KNOW THEY'RE ABOUT TO INVADE THE EAST AND THAT LEAVES YOU NO CHOICE.

WHATEVER CARDS YOU HAVE LEFT, IT'S TIME TO PLAY 'EM.

HAWKINS...

SHOULDN'T WE, UH, GET THIS LITTLE EXPERIMENT GOING?

ALL SET HERE.

HOPE I WASN'T INTERRUPTING ANYTHING...

JUST GETTING TO KNOW EACH OTHER.

HE SINGLE-HANDEDLY WIPED OUT TWENTY-THREE CITIES.

WHAT EXACTLY DO YOU WANT A GUY LIKE THAT TO KNOW ABOUT YOU?

VROOOOOOOOOOM BZZZZZZT

"IT'S MAJOR PETRELLA, HE'S BEEN KILLED."

THEY FOUND HIS HUMVEE SHOT UP JUST OUTSIDE OF TOWN. RUMORS ARE IT WAS ROAD AGENTS.

ROAD AGENTS? THERE HAVEN'T BEEN ROAD AGENTS OUTSIDE OF TOWN FOR MONTHS.

I KNOW. IT DOESN'T MAKE ANY SENSE.

WHO'S THAT WITH BECK?

INVESTIGATORS FROM CHEYENNE. PETRELLA DIED UNDER BECK'S WATCH. THEY'RE HOLDING HIM RESPONSIBLE.

THEY DON'T THINK BECK HAD SOMETHING TO DO WITH IT?

ALL THEY KNOW IS PETRELLA LEFT TOWN IN A HURRY, AND BECK LET HIM GO WITHOUT AN ESCORT.

THEY'RE SUSPICIOUS. AND UNTIL THEY GET ANSWERS, BECK'S GONNA STAY IN THE HOT SEAT.

IF BECK TAKES THE BLAME FOR THIS, HE'LL LOSE HIS COMMAND.

AND IF THAT HAPPENS, ALL THE A.S.A. COMMANDERS THAT HE TURNED WILL RUN FOR THE HILLS.

EVERYTHING WE'VE FOUGHT FOR WILL CRUMBLE.

WE NEED TO FIND PETRELLA'S KILLER BEFORE IT'S TOO LATE.

I THINK I KNOW WHERE TO START...

CHA·CHUNK

FOLLOW ME.

CC?

CC41

COMMAND AND CONTROL. FALLOUT SHELTER.

ONE OF EIGHT I MAINTAINED IN SECRET WHILE WORKING FOR J&R.

APPARENTLY, NOT AS SECRET AS YOU THOUGHT.

WHAT'S GOING ON HERE, SMITH?

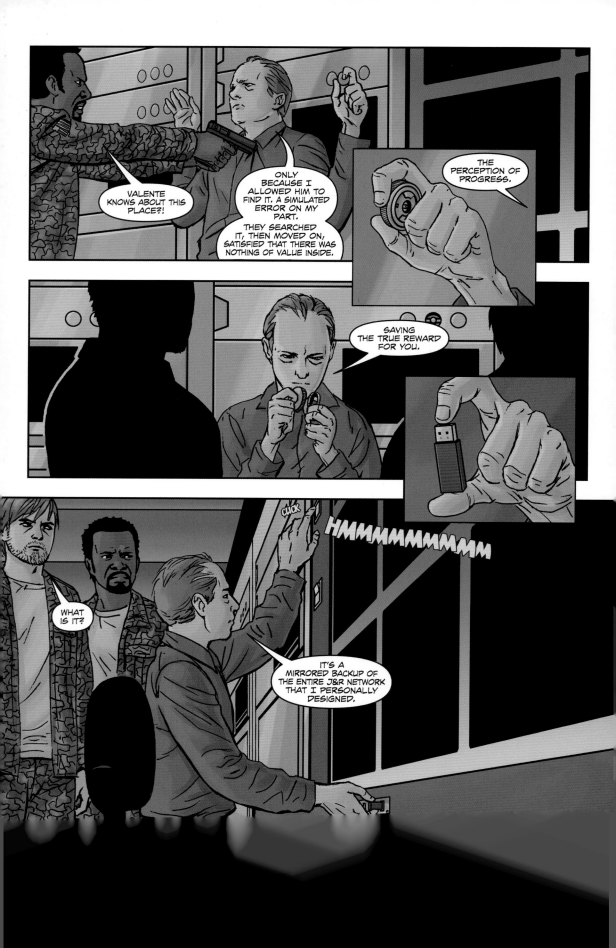

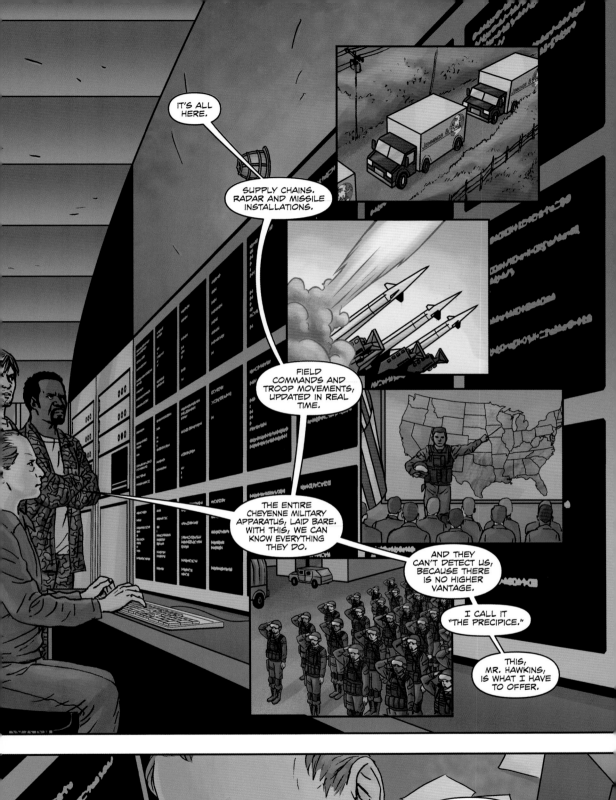

IT'S ALL HERE.

SUPPLY CHAINS. RADAR AND MISSILE INSTALLATIONS.

FIELD COMMANDS AND TROOP MOVEMENTS, UPDATED IN REAL TIME.

THE ENTIRE CHEYENNE MILITARY APPARATUS, LAID BARE. WITH THIS, WE CAN KNOW EVERYTHING THEY DO.

AND THEY CAN'T DETECT US, BECAUSE THERE IS NO HIGHER VANTAGE.

I CALL IT "THE PRECIPICE."

THIS, MR. HAWKINS, IS WHAT I HAVE TO OFFER.

I HOPE YOU'RE NOT DISAPPOINTED.

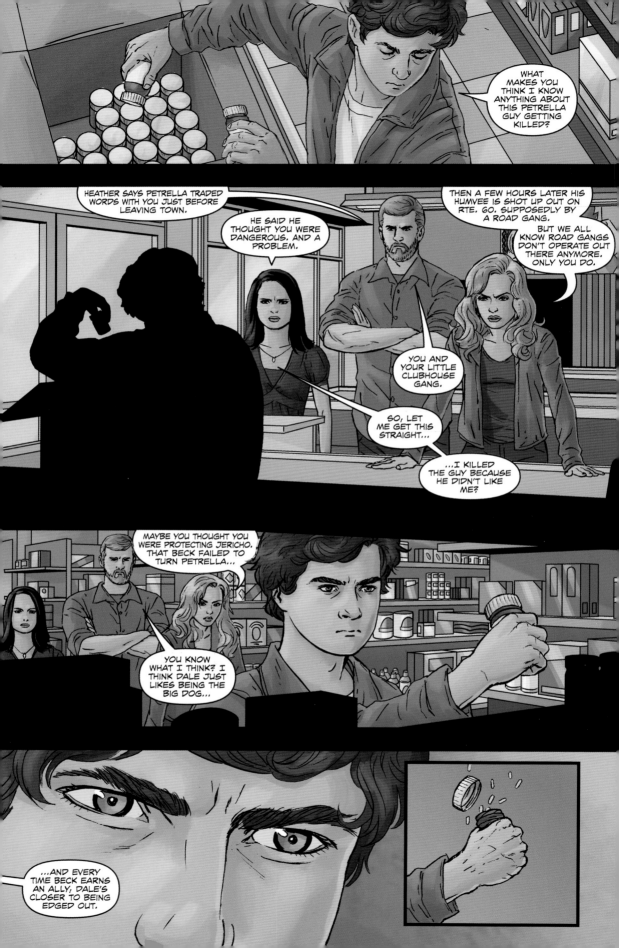

WELL?

YOU WERE RIGHT. DALE LIED TO ME.

WE'RE SORRY, SKYLAR.

I DON'T KNOW WHAT YOU WANT FROM ME.

I WON'T HELP YOU PUT DALE IN PRISON.

WE'RE NOT ASKING YOU TO. WE JUST WANT TO SAVE BECK. THAT'S ALL.

TACOMA BRIDGE. WE HAVE TO HURRY.

THANK YOU.

WHAT IS IT?

SECURITY ALARM AT ONE OF OUR OLD COMMAND AND CONTROL BUNKERS.

SOMEONE'S TRIPPED IT.

REYNOLDS...

HE WENT BACK FOR SOMETHING...

WE CAN HAVE AN S.F. TEAM THERE IN FIFTEEN MINUTES.

NO. WE'VE BEEN DOWN THAT ROAD.

OUR PRESIDENT WANTS A MORE *DEFINITIVE* OUTCOME.

"A BIRD IN THE HAND, AS THEY SAY."

WHOOOOSSSSHH

IT'S IMPRESSIVE, SMITH. LEAVES ME WITH ONE QUESTION, THOUGH.

WHICH IS...

IF I HAVE THE PRECIPICE, WHAT DO I NEED YOU FOR?

A FAIR POINT. UNFORTUNATELY, I'M THE ONLY PERSON WITH THE PERMISSIONS TO ACCESS IT. AND THEY'RE PROGRAMMED TO CHANGE DAILY.

I SUPPOSE YOU COULD TORTURE ME FOR THEM, BUT...

I DOUBT YOU HAVE THE TIME.

UH GUYS...

WHAT IS IT?

AN ORDER JUST WENT OUT. COORDINATES FOR A PREDATOR DRONE BOMBING.

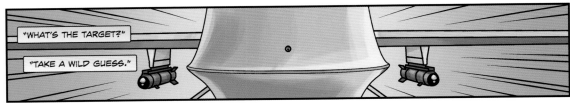

"WHAT'S THE TARGET?"

"TAKE A WILD GUESS."

THEY KNOW WE'RE HERE?

THE ENTRANCE WAS WIRED IN CASE I EVER CAME BACK.

YOU SET US UP...

IN A MANNER OF SPEAKING. I'D EXPLAIN, BUT...

...WE DON'T HAVE MUCH TIME.

CONGRATULATIONS, GENTLEMEN. YOU'RE OFFICIALLY GHOSTS.

THE TUNNEL WE USED IS COLLAPSED. IN VALENTE'S EYES, WHATEVER WE CAME HERE TO RETRIEVE IS DESTROYED, ALONG WITH US.

"THE PERCEPTION OF PROGRESS."

LEAVING US FREE TO CONTINUE OUR MISSION.

THAT'S WHERE YOU'RE WRONG, SMITH.

WE DON'T HAVE A MISSION.

I DO. YOU'RE JUST A TOOL, TO SEE THAT IT GETS DONE.

DON'T EVER KEEP SOMETHING FROM ME AGAIN.

SIR, YOU'RE GONNA WANT TO COME OUTSIDE.

WHAT'S GOING ON?

THEY FOUND PETRELLA'S KILLER. AND THE GUN HE USED.

HOW?

HOW DO YOU THINK?

YOU TOLD THEM?

IT'S THE TRUTH, ISN'T IT?

SKYLAR... HE WAS FOLLOWING ORDERS. MY ORDERS.

THAT'S NOT WHAT HE'LL TELL THEM.

"HE'LL TELL THEM HE HATES THE A.S.A., ALWAYS HAS. JENNINGS AND RALL TOOK OVER HIS BUSINESS, PUSHED HIM OUT. EVEN THREATENED HIM WITH JAIL IF HE DIDN'T GO ALONG.

"HE WAS DRUNK THAT NIGHT. WANTED SOME PAYBACK. WANTED *TO HURT*.

"AT FIRST, IT FELT GOOD. BUT THE GUILT WAS TOO MUCH.

"AS MUCH AS HE TOLD HIMSELF THOSE SOLDIERS DESERVED IT, HE KNEW, DEEP DOWN, THAT HE'D DONE WRONG. THAT ALL HE'D DONE WAS PUT THE PEOPLE HE LOVED IN DANGER.

"THAT'S WHAT HE'LL TELL THEM. NOTHING MORE."

THAT'S ALL HE'LL SAY BECAUSE *HIS FAMILY* IS STILL HERE. HIS WIFE AND KIDS.

THERE'S A WAR COMING, AND HE KNOWS THEY'RE GONNA NEED *OUR HELP* TO SURVIVE.

IT'S WHAT I'VE BEEN SAYING ALL THIS TIME, DALE.

ALL WE HAVE IS EACH OTHER.

MAJOR...?

THEY'VE CLOSED THE CASE. I'M TO RESUME MY COMMAND OF JERICHO, EFFECTIVE IMMEDIATELY.

MORE IMPORTANTLY, THE OTHER A.S.A. COMMANDERS CAN REST EASY. THEY KNOW I'M STILL IN POWER, AND THAT I DIDN'T KILL PETRELLA.

OUR COALITION IS INTACT.

I DON'T KNOW HOW YOU DID IT, BUT... THANK YOU.

I'M SURE I DON'T HAVE TO TELL YOU WHAT YOU SAVED TODAY.

NO, YOU DON'T.

BZZZZZZT

NOW WHAT?

IT'S HAWKINS.

"ANY SIGN OF THEIR BODIES?"

BZZZZZZT

CHAPTER SIX

SO WHAT DO WE TELL THEM? WHEN THEY ASK WHO HE IS?

THE TRUTH...

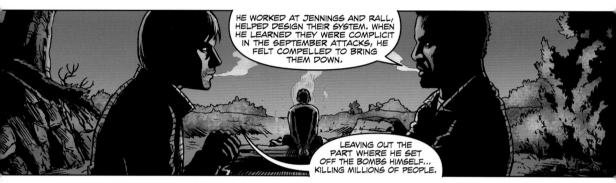

HE WORKED AT JENNINGS AND RALL, HELPED DESIGN THEIR SYSTEM. WHEN HE LEARNED THEY WERE COMPLICIT IN THE SEPTEMBER ATTACKS, HE FELT COMPELLED TO BRING THEM DOWN.

LEAVING OUT THE PART WHERE HE SET OFF THE BOMBS HIMSELF... KILLING MILLIONS OF PEOPLE.

WE DIDN'T COME ALL THIS WAY TO SEE HIM STRUNG UP, JAKE. WHAT HE KNOWS IS TOO IMPORTANT.

WHATEVER YOU HAVE TO DO TO MAKE PEACE WITH THAT... DO IT NOW.

I'M GOING TO SCOUT THE RENDEZVOUS POINT.

BE SURE TO PUT THE FIRE OUT.

AS YOU CAN SEE, I'VE BEEN BUSY SINCE YOU LEFT.

EACH OF THESE PINS REPRESENTS AN A.S.A. COMMANDER WHO HAS SECRETLY PLEDGED TO JOIN OUR CAUSE.

ALL TOLD, THAT'S CLOSE TO TEN BATTALIONS.

ALL OF THEM SWAYED BY THE EVIDENCE YOU GAVE ME, HAWKINS.

I WANT TO SAY I'M SORRY. FOR CHASING YOU OUT OF TOWN.

I JUST WASN'T READY TO SEE THE TRUTH.

GLAD YOU FINALLY CAME AROUND.

THE RESISTANCE COMMANDERS ARE STANDING BY ON THE SECURE TELECOM.

THEY'RE ANXIOUS TO HEAR WHAT MR. REYNOLDS HERE HAS TO SAY.

LET'S NOT KEEP THEM WAITING...

ACTUALLY, MR. HAWKINS, LET ME HANDLE THIS.

YOU AND JAKE HAVE MORE PRESSING BUSINESS...

"JAKE, THEY NEED YOU DOWNSTAIRS AT BAILEY'S."

NEED A HAND?

ROBERT?

DAD!

I'M SO GLAD YOU'RE HOME.

ME, TOO, PAL. WHERE'S YOUR SISTER?

SAM, WHY DON'T YOU GO UPSTAIRS AND PLAY FOR A BIT? MOMMY NEEDS TO TALK TO DADDY IN PRIVATE.

WHERE IS SHE, DARCY? WHERE'S ALLISON?

BEFORE I SAY ANY MORE, I JUST WANT YOU TO KNOW...

...I TRIED TO STOP HER.

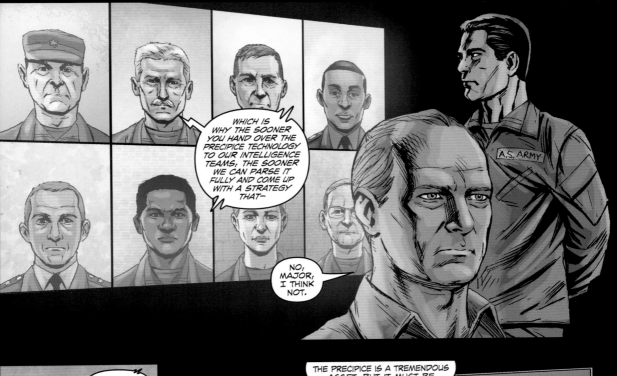

WHICH IS WHY THE SOONER YOU HAND OVER THE PRECIPICE TECHNOLOGY TO OUR INTELLIGENCE TEAMS, THE SOONER WE CAN PARSE IT FULLY AND COME UP WITH A STRATEGY THAT—

NO, MAJOR, I THINK NOT.

YOU THINK NOT?

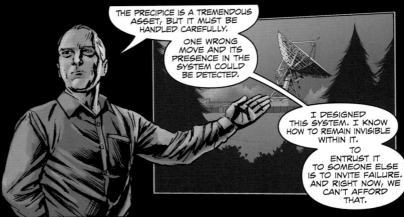

THE PRECIPICE IS A TREMENDOUS ASSET, BUT IT MUST BE HANDLED CAREFULLY.

ONE WRONG MOVE AND ITS PRESENCE IN THE SYSTEM COULD BE DETECTED.

I DESIGNED THIS SYSTEM. I KNOW HOW TO REMAIN INVISIBLE WITHIN IT.

TO ENTRUST IT TO SOMEONE ELSE IS TO INVITE FAILURE. AND RIGHT NOW, WE CAN'T AFFORD THAT.

USING THE PRECIPICE, I HAVE UNCOVERED THE LOCATION OF FIVE MAJOR SATELLITE STATIONS WITHIN THE A.S.A.

THESE STATIONS ARE ESSENTIAL TO COORDINATING THE A.S.A. DRONE BOMBING RAIDS.

TAKE THEM OUT, AND WE DISRUPT CHEYENNE'S PLAN FOR A BLOODLESS TAKEOVER, BUYING US A FEW PRECIOUS WEEKS.

THIS IS OUR ONLY STRATEGY.

SURVIVAL.

NOW... I SUGGEST WE GET MOVING.

NEW BERN, KANSAS

"HOW'S OUR PRISONER? IS HE SOFTENED UP?"

YEAH... MANNY WENT A LITTLE OVERBOARD.

GUY'S TOUGH, MR. CONSTANTINO. MIGHT BE A WHILE BEFORE HE'S READY TO TALK.

HE WAS HEADED TO BECK IN JERICHO. AT NIGHT, SO IT MUST BE URGENT. IF WE CAN FIND OUT WHY, HE COULD BE A VALUABLE TRADE...

A TRADE FOR WHAT?

INFORMATION. IT'S TIME WE FOUND OUT WHAT'S GOING ON IN THAT TOWN.

ALL DUE RESPECT, BOSS, BUT WHAT'S TO FIND OUT?

THEY REBELLED AFTER THAT RICHMOND GIRL GOT KILLED, BECK CRACKED DOWN, IT'S BEEN QUIET EVER SINCE.

YOU ASK ME, THEY ROLLED OVER.

TRUST ME, AS LONG AS JOHNSTON GREEN'S FAMILY STILL LIVES THERE, NO ONE'S ROLLED OVER.

IF THINGS ARE QUIET, IT'S FOR A REASON. AND WE'RE NOT GONNA GET ANSWERS SITTING OUT HERE IN THE DARK.

I'VE BEEN WAITING FOR THE RIGHT OLIVE BRANCH. THIS GUY MAY BE IT.

WHATEVER YOU SAY, BOSS...

...I'LL TELL MANNY TO STEP IT UP.

JAKE?

HEY. GO BACK TO SLEEP. IT'S OKAY.

SOMETHING'S ON YOUR MIND.

IT'S NOTHING. IT'S JUST I'VE BEEN WAITING SO LONG TO GET HOME.

NOW I'M HERE AND... I STILL CAN'T TAKE IT EASY.

OKAY, WELL...

I HAVE SCHOOL IN THE MORNING.

WHENEVER YOU WANT TO TALK ABOUT WHAT'S *REALLY* ON YOUR MIND... GIVE ME A SHAKE.

I'M STILL A BAD LIAR, HUH?

THE WORST. IT'S WHY I LOVE YOU.

JAKE?

BACK IN A FEW.

DON'T WAIT UP.

SHOULDN'T YOU BE WITH YOUR FAMILY?

SHOULDN'T YOU?

CAME TO SEE BECK. SOMETHING TELLS ME THAT'S WHY YOU'RE HERE, TOO.

WE MADE A MISTAKE, HAWKINS. WE NEED TO TELL THEM WHO SMITH IS.

WE NEED TO TELL THE TRUTH.

"I KNOW YOU THINK HE'S ON OUR SIDE NOW. THAT HE WANTS WHAT WE WANT. BUT WE CAN'T TRUST HIM."

"DOESN'T MATTER, JAKE."

"WE'RE AT WAR NOW. ALL THAT MATTERS IS WHAT HE CAN GIVE US."

"BUT THAT'S WHAT SCARES ME. THE MORE HE HELPS US, THE MORE POWERFUL HE GETS."

"IF WE DON'T TELL SOMEONE NOW, WE MAY NEVER HAVE THE CHANCE. NO ONE WILL BELIEVE US. THEY WON'T WANT TO BELIEVE US."

"JAKE, THIS IS YOUR LAST CHANCE."

UNIT TO COMMAND. ALL EXPLOSIVES ARE IN PLACE.

STEP AWAY FROM THE DOOR. I'M THROUGH ASKING.

CONTACT IN FIVE... FOUR... THREE...

GET YOUR HAND OFF ME, HAWKINS.

...TWO... ONE...

BECK'S A GOOD MAN, BUT HE'S JUST A SOLDIER. SOLDIERS NEED THINGS TO BE SIMPLE.

IF YOU TELL HIM ABOUT SMITH, HE MAY WELL KEEP THE SECRET. BUT THE KNOWLEDGE WILL PARALYZE HIM.

HE'LL QUESTION EVERY MOVE, EVERY ORDER SMITH SUGGESTS. WE CAN'T AFFORD THAT. SO WE LIE.

YOU'VE GOT IT ALL FIGURED OUT, DON'T YOU, HAWKINS?

BUT YOU KNOW WHAT I THINK?

LIES ARE WHAT GOT US HERE IN THE FIRST PLACE.

HE THINKS I CAN'T CONTROL SMITH.

HE'S WRONG.

HE THINKS I'LL GIVE IN.

I WON'T.

MY DAUGHTER'S OUT THERE, JAKE.

ALLISON. SHE VOLUNTEERED, AS AN AID WORKER. SHE'S ON HER WAY TO THE BLUE LINE RIGHT NOW.

I CAN'T GET HER BACK, JAKE. SHE'S GONNA BE THERE WHEN THE BULLETS FLY.

FOR ALL I KNOW SHE'LL BE THE ONE SHOOTING THEM.

WHATEVER I CAN DO TO STOP THIS WAR, I WILL DO IT.

THAT'S AN AFFIRMATIVE.

ALL FIVE TARGETS ARE DESTROYED.

CONGRATULATIONS, EVERYONE. THE MISSION IS A SUCCESS.

THREE CHEERS FOR DAVID REYNOLDS.

CLAP CLAPCLAP CLAP CLAP CLAP CLAP

HAPPY TO HELP.

CLAP CLAPCLAP CLAP CLAP CLAP CLAPCLAP CLAP CLAP CLAP

TO BE CONTINUED...

At first, when I heard about *Jericho*, I was like "nukes going off in this country, are they out of their minds?" But when the pilot aired, I was immediately hooked.

Jericho had the most original premise I had ever seen on TV. This show, about a little town in Kansas cut off from the rest of the world, had a rich and powerful story. While there was great mystery about who precipitated the attacks, the characters within the town itself are what resonated with me week after week.

Each character had such depth breathed into them by the genius writers, while the cast crafted each performance superbly. This show was something unique and special… until it was taken away from us.

I was devastated when I heard about the cancellation and knew we needed a rallying cry. Jake Green gave it to us as he cried out "NUTS" heading into battle at the end of Season One. At that moment, a TV revolution had begun.

The "Save *Jericho*" campaign and the 7-episode second season changed my life. Hearing from people around the world drove home the fact that in a life of swings and misses, I hit a home run with my efforts for *Jericho*. I could not believe it. Little old me did something to help bring back a TV series. Getting that second season was by far one of the greatest accomplishments of my life.

None of this could've happened without the community of *Jericho* fans. They are remarkable and I am honored to be a part of that family.

We are so proud of the Second Season and now seeing Season Three in a comic book series tells us one thing…

Jericho, in one form or another, will always live on…

Shaun O'Mac aka Shaun Daily

Shaun O'Mac is an internet radio broadcaster who hosted the show TV TALK on blogtalkradio. Shaun was one of the first journalists to talk regularly about Jericho when it aired in September 2006, and his show created a home for fans to call in and discuss their favorite TV series. Shaun was also the figure that rallied the fans of Jericho to send nuts to CBS to bring the show back from cancellation. Shaun is an inspiration to all who fight for what they love.

ART GALLERY

BY SCOTT WEST

WANTED

BY THE ASA

ACTS OF TERRORISM

Jake Green

Robert Hawki...

Any Cooperation with the

Terrorists is a Federal Crim...

...ou have any information about the

...ersons, contact your local ASA offic...

...r nearst ASA Embassy or Consulate